FALLING FOR MIAMI

Jack Atherton

Boroughs
Publishing Group

www.BOROUGHSPUBLISHINGGROUP.com

PUBLISHER'S NOTE: This is a work of fiction. Names, characters, places and incidents either are the product of the author's imagination or are used fictitiously. Any resemblance to actual events, locales, business establishments or persons, living or dead, is coincidental. Boroughs Publishing Group does not have any control over and does not assume responsibility for author or third-party websites, blogs or critiques or their content.

FALLING FOR MIAMI
Copyright © 2019 John Atherton

ISBN 978-1-951055-14-1

For Aymsley, always

ACKNOWLEDGMENTS

I'd like to thank all the news stations that gave me the chance to learn the business, and also to my family who always give me the business.

Finally, heartfelt thanks to Michelle Klayman and her team at Boroughs Publishing Group for believing in this book and editing it thoroughly but gently.

FALLING FOR MIAMI

1

LIZZIE

I'm perched on top of the anchor desk in a dress so short ice skaters wouldn't be allowed to wear it at the Olympics. This is not my choice.

"Can I get a key on her face?" Harry Lutz is calling to Erin, our lighting tech, who's adjusting the overhead grid.

The studio's dim until a spotlight smacks me right in the eyes.

"Wider, please." Lutz smiles. It's more like a leer. "I want to frame Lizzie's whole lovely figure."

My fair to middling figure is already framed by this sheath of Saran wrap that Lutz picked out for me to wear. To keep the dress from riding up to my waist, I sit as rigid as one of those Egyptian statues, my knees so tightly locked I may never again be able to walk.

Lutz winks at me. "Okay, darling, go ahead and cross your legs."

Look, I'm far from being a prude. But come on. This isn't some game show where I'd be turning letters in five-inch Jimmy Choo stilettos. It's not an I-slept-with-my-boyfriend's-boss reality show where I'd be dressed for a fight. This is a newscast. And here I am, finally at the anchor desk in Miami, but instead of sitting behind the desk and anchoring, I'm draped on top of it like a piece of merchandise.

Maybe I'm supposed to be flattered. Harry Lutz was flown down by the network to merchandise me for their Miami station, WTAN. I know, the call letters TAN are unfortunate. Whenever we get beat on a story, the competition jeers, *"WTAN is off working on its tan again."* So we try not to get beat on stories. And that's been easier since we were bought by the United Broadcasting Network. UBN has pumped in a load of money, and now it expects to earn that money back with higher ratings.

Which brings us to Harry Lutz. He's never won any journalism awards. Never run a newsroom. He's a consultant whose claim to fame is that he boosted ratings in LA by turning reporters into pin-ups. Harry himself is no sex object. His paunch is about to burst the buttons of his bright blue suit. His three-day beard doesn't look hip and grizzled. It looks like he's been guzzling booze from a bag. Yet it's his job to tell everyone how to speak, how to move, how to dress, and now, how to flirt with viewers like a single at a South Beach bar.

I'm single but not that desperate. So I keep my knees locked.

"Did you hear me, Lizzie? Please cross your legs."

"I heard you," Bob Beardsley drawls.

Bob has won journalism awards. He does run a newsroom. And our news director hails not from Miami, Florida, the land of surf and skin, but from Waco, Texas, the home of HGTV's Jo and Chip Gaines. Men there still retain a sense of chivalry, especially when they have three grown kids—one of them my age, twenty-five. Bob Beardsley is what fellow Texans call a long, tall drink of water, and he's normally about as placid. Now, though, when he walks into my light, he's about to boil over.

"Why are you trying to cheapen one of my best reporters?"

And Bob has a posse.

Erin clambers down her ladder. Her wire-rimmed granny glasses and apple cheeks remind me of my third grade teacher, but under her overalls, Erin is a weightlifter. Lenny Fogle is not. Our floor director steps out from the shadows, ready to rumble, though he's got to be pushing seventy. Together, with Bob, they converge on the consultant.

I can stand up for myself, but I'm grateful. These good people like me and I like them. Still, Lutz is armed with the network's blessing. So to avoid trouble for everyone, I cross my legs as demurely as Queen Elizabeth crosses her ankles. Because, you see, this is my big break. I'm draped on this desk rehearsing for my debut as WTAN's featured consumer reporter. As head of our new Help Center, I'll be leading a roomful of volunteers answering consumer complaints. And I'll be teaming with a Florida assistant attorney general who's so handsome he should've been on TV long ago.

Trouble is, you forget his face because Nicholas Harris, Esq., is a total ass.

That sounds awful, especially after what I've been saying about Harry Lutz. Truth is, I get along with everyone. My hometown is Cincinnati, Ohio. We may not be Texas Rangers, but about all the people I grew up with are Midwestern nice. So I'm the one who brings morning donuts, who never complains about assignments or vacation schedules or when other reporters—including guys— borrow my makeup and don't replace the tops.

But here's what happened two days ago. I called Mr. Harris at his Consumer Protection Office.

Ring-ring, ring-ring, ring-ring.

Come on. Pick up.

Ring-ring.

"Harris."

That's it? That's his greeting to consumers with a problem?

"Hello," I sparkle. "This is Lizzie Lomax. Nick Harris?"

Silence.

"Hello?" I ask.

"Nicholas. Yes."

"Sorry." Nettled but unfazed. "I'm excited that we're going to be working together."

"That's not settled yet," he says.

His voice matches his picture. He was scowling in the photo and this was on LinkedIn, not some government directory.

I ask, "What do you mean?"

What the hell does he mean? We're supposed to be shooting our first story in three days.

Nicholas Harris, Esq. sighs. "The Attorney General, Leland Davis, spoke with your station about this, but he never spoke with me until this morning. Apparently, Mr. Davis is unaware that we're in the middle of several major investigations here at the Miami office. I don't have time to go on television with you to advise people that if they want to return merchandise, they ought to save their receipts."

Now I'm the one who says nothing.

He finally asks, "Are you still there?"

"Yes, Mr. Harris. Well, I'm sorry there's been a misunderstanding. I value the work you do, and I'm sorry you don't value mine. With your help, or the help of someone from your office, we're also hoping to pursue major investigations. But we don't want to trouble anyone who views us as an annoyance."

"I'm glad you feel that way, Ms. Lomax. Attorney General Davis and I will be meeting tomorrow in Tallahassee, the state capital—"

"I know the state capital. Do you know the capital of Vermont?" My mom isn't a teacher for nothing.

"I beg your pardon?"

"Well, I hope you and your boss will get all this straightened out."

"Thank you, Ms. Lomax. Anything else?"

Yes. No. Oh, why not. "One more thing, Mr. Harris. Did my sister really go out with you?"

Silence.

"That was a long time ago," he says, stiffly.

I suspect he kissed Karen stiffly.

"When you must've been a different person. Thank you for your valuable time, Mr. Harris." And I hang up.

Speaking of my sister, when I say this Help Center is my big break, I'm not bragging. How could I, when every Thursday you can watch Karen on the network's primetime news magazine? Still, having a consumer franchise in Miami is bigger than anything I imagined possible five years ago when I started interning and then writing part-time at a Cincinnati station. And bigger than I could've hoped three years ago, when I snagged my first reporting job up I-75 in Dayton.

You might be wondering, if your sister's made it to the network, why is reporting in Miami such an unlikely step for you? Because I'm not my older sister. If you saw me next to Karen, or if you talked with us, you would agree. Karen Lomax is stunning. Five-foot nine, auburn waves with ice blue eyes of a ravenous young wolf. Beyond all that, Karen is brilliant. She studied languages at Vanderbilt and Oxford and now speaks French, Spanish, and I kid you not, Arabic. That's what got her assigned by UBN—after a brief stint in Houston—to Iraq, where Karen covered the war against ISIS.

By contrast, and it's quite a contrast, I'm five-foot two. I have flyaway mousy brown hair. On especially humid days—that's every day in Miami—my hair looks like a cobweb, so I pull it back. My eyes are a bluish-greenish blah that my darling mother says, evoke the sea. More like brackish water on a cloudy day. I speak a little *Español* and ungrammatical English. And I'm ashamed to tell you what launched me from Dayton to Miami, because it's a heartbreaking story that confirms all you ever thought about reporters exploiting tragedies.

One day in July, I was up in a helicopter outside Dayton, with a photographer named Dave Schreiber, shooting aerial video of highway construction. Pounding rain had flooded our normally pokey rivers and turned them into rapids. But the rain cleared and it was now sunny.

We spotted a bus filled with campers, crossing a small bridge. Suddenly, the bus skidded off the bridge and plunged into the river. Our pilot, Corey Sack, nosedived toward the bus, now half-submerged. Twelve- and thirteen-year-old children were bobbing up and down in the fast-moving current. Half of them swam to the shore. With Dave shooting it all, Corey showed me how to use his hoist to fish the other kids out of the river as they grasped his line. Then he gently dropped each of them onto the dry bank. We rescued seven campers in all.

All but the last. She was struggling to stay afloat, so we tried reeling her in early, but she kept losing her grip on the line. When Emily was the only one left—we later learned that was her name— Corey dipped the helicopter as close to the water as he could. I reached out, but Corey yelled that it was too dangerous. Not out of anger. Anguish.

Dave turned off his camera and joined Corey and me begging Emily to hold onto the line. A counselor dived into the river and nearly drowned struggling to reach her. But Emily lost her grip and drowned. We saw her go under.

Dave's video went viral. All the networks, broadcast and cable, played it mercilessly. And that mercilessly played video, along with my tearful live shots, prompted calls from Cincinnati, from my sister's old station in Houston, and from Miami.

Emily was dead and I was in demand. That's the business. So maybe I don't have any right to look down my nose at Harry Lutz.

2

NICK

I'm staring at a Seminole Indian. You'd think Attorney General Leland Davis might prefer another statue. Say, a blindfolded woman holding the scales of justice. But this is Florida State country, and that Seminole's the school mascot.

"Made good time." The AG smirks. "You still driving that James Bond wannabe? I told you, boy, get an American car."

My '88 Jaguar is a classic, with a hood so long it looks like it's pouncing.

"Okay." Davis grimaces. "I assume you didn't come to consult me about what car you ought to buy."

"No."

"I know why you're here." Leland Davis is the kind of guy who always knows, even when he doesn't. "You're pretending you don't want to be a TV star."

"Do you want to be a TV star?"

"Sure. I just don't have the time."

"I don't have the time, either."

"You'll make time." Davis flashes a smile that guys at his rival school would appreciate—a menacing Florida Gator smile. "Look and listen. This is going to be superb publicity for the Department, especially Consumer Protection. UBN is setting up a whole new wing at that station for volunteers. And being on TV will do you plenty of good. Ask your mom. Her black robe doesn't come from Santa Claus, or even the governor. A judge needs votes, like me. And the key is name recognition."

"Sir."

"Oh, we're going to get pissy," Davis says.

"Do you know what I'm working on right now?"

"Of course. It's on the front page of every paper." He's being sarcastic.

"No, it's not," I say. "That's the point. Television doesn't care about fraudulent debt collection, even when I offer them a grandma who's about to lose her home. We send out press releases, they treat them like junk mail. We're looking to collect more than a million dollars in refunds in Miami-Dade alone."

"And if you're in charge at that Help Zone—"

"Help Center."

"If you're one of the people calling the shots," the AG says, with mock patience, "you can put phony debt collectors on television. Look, Nick." Davis leans in over his desk and for the first time seems almost friendly. "You're a sneaky bastard. You play everything too close to the vest. But you've got the track record. You've got the connections. They tell me you've got the presence."

"Presence?"

"Okay, they said you've got the looks. I look like a bullfrog, so it's a good thing I don't have the time. But you can help your colleagues up here and little old ladies down there. You might get so popular that the network will hire you away from us. And pay you enough to buy a new ride. You never asked what would *truly* impress the women."

"What?"

"Luxor Montana pickup, boy. Full-size. You weren't lucky enough to go here, but paint it FSU colors. Garnet and gold. That's good enough for me, and it's sure as hell good enough for you."

<u>3</u>

LIZZIE

"Nick Harris?" Karen asks.

"He introduced himself on the phone to me as Nicholas," I say. "Stiff as a corpse. But I Googled him, and yeah, everyone else calls him Nick."

"That could be him."

"I've got it." Mom is holding Karen's Vanderbilt yearbook up to the camera.

It's Sunday and we're on our Skype call. Me in Miami, Karen in New York, Mom and Dad back home in Ohio. Dad says three-way Skyping beats Cincinnati's three-way chili, but mostly he shies away from the camera. Karen and I hear his comments from the peanut gallery while he watches a Reds or Bengals game.

"Yup, that's Nick," Karen says. "How many other guys wear bowties for their school pictures?"

"What was he?" I laugh. "A continuing education student?"

"No, he's my age. But… formal."

"It's the ones who bottle it up that you've got to watch out for," Dad yells.

Mom is examining the yearbook. "Are there any pictures of you together?"

Karen shakes her head. "We weren't a big thing. Well, actually, Nick was, because of his father. I don't want to get into that."

"What?" Dad calls out.

Karen goes on, "Has he asked about me?"

"No," I reply.

Karen seems put out. "Have you actually met him yet?"

"Only on the phone. He's trying to get out of working with us."

"Why?" Mom wants to know.

Now she's being protective, thinking this longhaired guy in a bowtie could be sabotaging my career.

"Nicholas Harris says his own cases are more important," I explain. "But his boss, the Attorney General, told him to come to the station tomorrow to see the setup."

I want to tell them that the Help Center looks terrific, but it's modest compared to Karen's studio.

"The hell with him," Dad hollers over the football game. "Find someone else."

I can see the TV in the background, but Dad hasn't yet made an appearance.

"Daddy," I yell, "get up and let us see you."

"Bengals are on a great drive. Five-yard line."

"Daddy," Karen calls. "Are you hiding because you're off your diet?"

Mom says nothing, but she picks up the laptop and focuses on a bowl big enough to serve the whole family. It's overflowing with popcorn and candy.

"Cindy," Dad squawks. "What're you doing?"

"Investigative reporting."

"Don't you know the government records everything on that camera and stores it in Utah?"

"Well," Mom says, resignedly, "the Mormons will get a thrill out of seeing how we live."

"Not for long," Karen says. "Not if you won't quit killing yourself. I'm not kidding."

Silence. Dad fears Karen more than Mom. We all do.

Mom isn't unkind. She hasn't shown us Dad sprawled on his Barca Lounge. I'm not unkind either, so I change the subject.

"Why did you and Nicholas—"

"Nick," Karen interrupts. "Call him Nick."

"He may insist that I call him Mr. Harris. Or Mr. Assistant Attorney General. Why did you break up?"

"He's very good looking," Mom says.

"It was never serious. We went out for, I don't know, two months maybe, senior year. I was heading to England. He was going to law school."

"Yale," I say.

"Really?" Mom's impressed.

Part of her job, besides teaching English, is helping high school kids prepare for the SATs.

"Yale is full of lefties." Dad's turned down the sound so we can all hear this. "Did you know they have a *sex week* at Yale so students can *explore* all kinds of *alternative…*"

We know Dad's on a roll when he puts air quotes around every other word. Lefties don't sit well with Dad. He's a Desert Storm vet and a cop.

"Well," Karen says, "I don't think Nick Harris had anything to learn at Yale except the law."

"Oh, really," Mom drawls.

She's pretty chill for someone devoted to Jane Austen.

Embarrassed, Dad turns up the sound so you'd think *we're* on the five-yard line.

"How's Kwami?" I ask.

Karen didn't sound comfortable talking about Nicholas. Nick. Whatever.

"Well," Karen huffs. "You'll be hearing about that tomorrow. Or maybe tonight."

"He's going to propose tonight?" Mom almost shrieks.

Me, too.

Mom likes Kwami Thomas. He's been to Cincinnati twice to visit. Everyone at Western Hills High School, including parents, came out to watch this bashful but alarmingly tall guy scrimmage with the basketball team. Mom, and of course Dad, saw him open the season at Madison Square Garden when they stayed at Karen's place a couple weeks ago. They also traveled, without Karen, to see the Knicks play in Indianapolis. So it's no surprise that—

"Mom, it's only been three months."

"Sweetie, I'm not pushing you."

"And now." Karen pauses.

Not for dramatic effect. She seems… I'm not sure. Not so much hurt as confused.

"I know you liked him."

"Don't you like him?" Mom asks.

"Yes. Yes, but it was never serious. Whatever you read."

"A guy comes to the house, from New York." Dad lumbers in front of the camera. "Twice. Stirs up the whole town. Seemed serious to me."

He did put on weight. Even after a triple bypass.

"Dan," Mom warns.

"I'm just saying. It was only a couple months, so that's fine with me. Nobody wants to see you rushing into anything."

"Anyway, I don't know how you find time to date." Mom says. And to change the subject she teasingly raises a copy of *Us Weekly* in front of the camera. "She looked even prettier on your show. And still so down-to-earth."

The magazine cover shows the Duchess of Sussex. Karen snagged her first American TV interview as a mom. Harry and Baby Archie ducked it, but hey. Karen met Meghan Markel when she was still doing *Suits*. They're not BFFs and Karen didn't go to the wedding, but they've stayed in touch and this was a *really* nice favor.

"We were watching her yesterday," Mom says, "on the Hallmark Channel. An old movie. Honey, what was the name of it?"

Dad's moved back to his throne. "How should I know?" he calls back.

"He knows all too well."

Mom explains to us in a loud whisper, "That football game is on to keep up appearances. Whenever I walk into the room, your father is clicking away from his Hallmark movies."

Dad storms back into view. This must've frightened the Iraqis, but Mom's unperturbed and stifling a giggle.

"I do not watch Hallmark movies."

"I think it's sweet," I say. "You're a romantic, Dad."

"For crying out—didn't you ever hear of channel surfing? If I land on Bravo, do you think I want to be a Real Housewife of Beverly Hills?"

To change the subject I ask my sister, "What are you working on now, Kary?"

We always called her Kary, but Mom stopped after Karen went on television. I'm still Lizzie. Our family never pulls out kitchen knives or anything, but it seems I'm always changing the subject. Maybe that's why the knives stay in the drawer. Kidding. We're great.

"They've got me up your alley," Karen says. "I can't talk about it, but it's a consumer investigation. A serious one."

"If *Backstory* is investigating, it must be serious," Mom says, not meaning to belittle my local stories.

"We'll see. If this pans out, it could be explosive. Literally. Okay, gotta go. I'm meeting Lauren for a late brunch."

"I love you. Both of you." Mom blows kisses to Karen and to me.

"Me, too," Dad shouts.

"But not as much as Hallmark movies," I sing.

4

NICK

The Miami branch of the attorney general's office is on Brickell Avenue, which is spectacular. Colossal palm trees line the street that seems as wide as the Champs Elysees in Paris. And high-rises dwarf the trees. Each building's designed by famous architects. Some have holes in the center, others are round or all crazy angles, and taken together Brickell Avenue looks like Oz. It's not only Brickell. Seems everything in Miami gets sleeker and richer by the minute. Thank the weather. And no state income tax. That brings Northerners down faster than skiers trying to outrun an avalanche. Those transplants keep our office open. Southerners make do. Northerners sue.

There's nothing distinctive about my space, apart from a photo of Mom in her judicial robes. The digital age is supposed to let us go paperless, so why do manila folders and cardboard boxes snake halfway to the ceiling? I'm fairly neat, but we're short of storage space in this branch, so the snake keeps growing. It's an annoyance until you remember that each of those files cost someone a lot more than annoyance, maybe even terror.

Really. The woman in the file at the top of the stack, Makayla Davis, bought a used car that lurched forward when she shifted gears, nearly hitting a little girl crossing the street. The dealer says her limited warranty doesn't cover the transmission repair, which Ms. Davis can't afford, so she called us. Small problem? Makayla Davis is now afraid to drive her car, and Brandy Cruz, the little girl, is now afraid of cars bigger than Hot Wheels.

Hmm. Maybe the Help Center would be interested. People should be warned about these limited warranties.

We're on the west side of Brickell Avenue, on the tenth floor, so no view of Biscayne Bay. As it happens though, WTAN's new studio is on the east side of Brickell, only a block from our building. For decades, WTAN broadcast from a converted movie theater downtown. As a first-grader, some friends and I got to visit their morning show. They brought in a chimp from Monkey Jungle and he climbed on my lap. My father arranged the visit. He golfed with Leon Tannenbaum, who owned the station before UBN bought it.

Reluctantly now, I'm walking across the street to their swanky new studio. It's right on the bay, with a wrap-around balcony I've seen from my boat. They use it for weather shots and outdoor interviews. News vehicles must be parked underground.

Once inside, there are glossy photos of the anchors, and weather and sports people. I give my name at the reception desk, which resembles a turquoise kidney-shaped pool. The network morning show is on TV sets across from the sofas, until the show breaks for a commercial for *Backstory*. And there's Karen.

***

LIZZIE

Well, there he is. Staring open-mouthed at my sister. I'll have to call Frank to mop up the drool. Really, Mr. Harris? Although, in that black lace number Kary's wearing, even Neil Patrick Harris would be drooling.

The problem is—let's get this out of the way and then forget about it—I'm drooling, too. Because Nicholas Harris, Esq., is no college kid. He's wearing Armani, or maybe something off the Goodwill rack that, on him, looks like Armani. He's still sporting a bow tie—blue, with dots that match his beige suit. But you know, now even the tie's kind of hot. Mr. Harris's sun-bleached blond hair is cut short. He has seams in his cheeks, a cleft in his chin. And his blue eyes are so bright they seem to be battery-powered. On top of all that, he's obviously been to the gym more recently than I have. Which is to say, sometime this year. And it's October.

I sneak behind him. "Why didn't you tell me you dated my sister?"

***

NICK

I turn as casually as I can and smile, thinly. "Is Karen still talking about me?"

"Absolutely. Duchess Meghan gushed about Prince Harry, but Kary couldn't stop talking about you. Yet she let you get away."

"Someday her prince will come."

"Oh, you're into Disney. Not many grown men admit that."

You're expecting me to tell you whether Lizzie Lomax is as beautiful as her sister. For people who don't see Miami TV, let me first tell you about her voice. It's soft and a little husky. I want to keep hearing her talk, even if it's all insults, but Lizzie turns and we're walking into the newsroom.

This is a long, narrow room with two-dozen or so low cubicles. They're crammed with desktop computers, personal photos, mugs, and bobbleheads. The lucky, maybe more senior reporters look out on Brickell Avenue. You can actually see my building from here. There's my window. The rest of the reporters and the producers nestle around the elevated assignment desk, where a harried, heavy-set guy seems to be holding three phones. TV monitors hang on the wall opposite that desk, all tuned to different channels—one to what looks like a live camera on a street corner. The newsroom doesn't face the water. That probably would be too distracting.

Only a handful of reporters are here. The others, I presume, are out in the field. One recognizes me, Patrick Diaz, from a lottery fraud case. Patrick's about my age, twenty-nine. His trademark is a fedora.

When I go over to shake hands, he grins. "Selling out, huh?"

"No, still on the government payroll."

Lizzie cuts in. "Meaning, we taxpayers still pay his salary. Let me show you the studio."

We walk past the assignment desk and I run into John McIntyre. Or, he staggers into me. No surprise to anyone in Miami that at half-past nine, Big John is already half-plastered. I remember reading in a gossip column that one morning John was supposed to judge a competition to see who caught the most hammerhead sharks. Fishermen piled them up on the South Pointe pier. When John showed up, he screamed and ran away, thinking the sharks were in pursuit.

Lizzie introduces me. "John, this is Nicholas Harris."

"Nick," I insist.

Did I really identify myself as Nicholas last week when Lizzie called? Why do I think she'll never let me forget that?

"Nicholas is an *assistant* attorney general." She emphasizes assistant, making it sound like junior. Or pretend.

"I didn't do it," John guffaws, raising his hands and booming with the classic Voice of God I've known since childhood.

I have to admit, kind of a thrill to hear it for the first time in person. John's wearing his trademark red suspenders, but one of them is hanging down by his side and a white bib is wrapped around his neck. I guess it's to protect his clothes from makeup.

Alicia Balart joins us. She's also wearing a bib. It makes her almond-shaped eyes seem even bigger, like Jasmine's in *Aladdin*. Wait a minute. Am I really hung up on Disney?

Lizzie introduces me to John's much younger co-anchor, and Alicia does a theatrical double take.

"Look at those blue eyes. Grrrrowl." She laughs and then shakes my shoulders. "This Help Center is going to be sensational." Alicia has a slight, delightful Cuban accent and her sentences race along. "My aunt has already volunteered. On condition that your first story is about her landlord, who is a prick." Alicia looks murderous.

Then she cracks up and the rest of us do, too.

"John and I have to go on the roof to shoot a promo." Alicia apologizes to Lizzie and to me.

The promo seems to be news to John.

"But go, show Nicky the studio," she urges Lizzie. Then Alicia stage whispers to me, "What an upgrade from the dump we used to have. The new anchor desk is fabulous. And Lizzie," she says, seriously, "I gave that pig Harry Lutz hell about embarrassing you. But you're going to be gorgeous. Look at her legs, Nicky. It's okay, we're not on TV. You can look. And that face. Nobody's going to be looking at me when Lizzie sits up there. So go see the studio. And then... " Alicia pauses for dramatic effect and salutes, "go see your new headquarters."

5

NICK

Since Alicia mentioned it, let me confirm. Lizzie Lomax is beautiful.

I had, of course, seen her on the air. Lizzie's the chief reason I watched. Hope this doesn't make me sound, I don't know... arrogant. Superior. Like an idiot. But local news usually isn't the news. Not the real news. I work in places like Little Havana and Little Haiti and I see people struggling to find jobs, to raise their kids, to pay doctor bills. And I don't see a lot of stories about that. Instead, it's all crime, weather, crime, sports and still more crime. And political scandals. With some *features* thrown in. I work in the attorney general's office. Crime is important. Ask any victim. But crime has root causes. Not having a job, not having adequate health care and schools, not having a father in the house.

Yet Lizzie seems to dig deeper. I remember watching her join Broward County deputies storming a crack house outside Fort Lauderdale. They'd secretly tracked one of the crackheads:

1) stealing everything from silver-plated goblets to Bibles from a storefront church,;

2) getting cash for the loot from a pawnshop, and

3) using that cash to score drugs.

Lizzie walked viewers through that seedy Bermuda Triangle, which encompassed a mere three blocks. When the crackhead was arrested, she and the station raised money for the little church. So yes, covering crime is important, when you don't treat it as spot news.

And I remember a feature Lizzie did on Mother's Day, about two mothers at Jackson Memorial Hospital. A new mom stood at the window of the neo-natal intensive care unit, praying for her preemie.

Then Lizzie took us to the hospital's oncology center. We saw a mother in her sixties undergoing chemo for a rare sort of cancer. She cried, telling Lizzie how her daughter, who was holding her hand, got her accepted into a clinical trial.

Lizzie made that story as beautiful as she looks. Large sea green eyes, chestnut hair that she lets fall naturally, not all swept up. Legs like Alicia said. And something I never saw with Karen. Lizzie Lomax almost always looks happy. What a smile. Although, I've only seen it on TV. We haven't hit it off. And as usual, I have only myself to blame.

Back at Vanderbilt, Karen never talked about her family. I didn't sense any tension. She simply didn't. However, when WTAN hired Lizzie, the newspapers mentioned the helicopter story where Lizzie helped save a busload of kids about to drown in a river, but one of them died. The papers also mentioned that Lizzie was Karen's sister.

For a while, watching Lizzie on the news—all right, stalking her on the news, because I'd monitor WTAN to catch a glimpse of her— I wondered if my attraction was a holdover from Karen. Then, when Lizzie called the attorney general's office in Tallahassee and Leland Davis referred her to me, well, it's strange. You see a person on TV, even if it is local television, and it's like meeting John and Alicia. I watch TV mostly on my phone. But the people are still bigger than life. John can be a buffoon, but he's still John McIntyre. And Lizzie is no buffoon.

So when she called, I was… I don't know what. Surprised. And shy. But it came off as arrogant. Like I was too busy to report on piddling consumer complaints. Like I was too important to do what she does for a living.

An old man chewing a wad of candy throws on the studio lights. There are plenty more overhead, but these are enough for me to see three gigantic video screens to the right of the curved double anchor desk. The desk has an illuminated blue panel in front and clear plexiglass on top. To the left is the green screen for Cris Robinson and the other meteorologists. You know how they use that, with the control room inserting weather maps.

The lights dim and all three video screens come alive with a nighttime shot of Miami's skyline. I've lived here all my life, yet it still takes my breath away.

"This is terrific," I tell Lizzie and the old man.

"Isn't it?" I think he says. The candy's dislodging his dentures.

"Lenny, meet Nick," Lizzie introduces us. "He's the guy from the AG's office."

Lenny offers me some halvah, a sticky bar made from sesame paste, Miami's favorite candy. I take it to be polite.

"Has he seen the Help Center yet?" Lenny asks. He's got a wonderful nasal voice, like one of the gamblers from *Guys and Dolls*.

"Next stop," Lizzie says.

"Where's the sports desk?" I ask.

Lizzie rolls her eyes. "Trying to show you're a regular guy? Even though you wear bowties and like cartoons?"

"I think that bowtie looks snazzy," Lenny says.

"Thanks."

"Hardly anyone wears a tie anymore. Back in the day, even at the dog track, half the guys wore ties. Including bowties."

Lizzie asks, "How many shirts did you lose at the track, Lenny? Not to mention ties."

Lenny shakes his head. "Too many. I won't even look at a Greyhound *bus* anymore. Good thing the tracks are gone. Go see the Help Center, Nick. Is it Nick?"

"Yeah. Good to meet you, Lenny."

"And don't let her talk you out of that bowtie."

Lizzie assures him, "I'm not talking Mr. Harris out of any clothing."

6

LIZZIE

To get to the Help Center, we have to walk through the sales department. What pays our salaries in television isn't taxpayers but commercials. Local TV used to be a cash cow. Most cities had only three or four stations. Your whole family huddled around the set in the living room and watched local news. Not anymore. So these folks in the sales department have to bust their butts.

I say hello to Rita. We often go to lunch together. And I introduce Nick to everyone.

As we walk down the long corridor to the Help Center, he asks, "Who was that guy Alicia says she chewed out because he embarrassed you?"

I'm too embarrassed to explain about Harry Lutz. "It's nothing. I'm handling it."

We open the door and now I'm proud. This used to be a storage room, but they've painted it soothing periwinkle, with the name Help Center in big yellow letters across the back wall and the phone number underneath. A long walnut table that can seat a dozen people stretches almost the whole length of the room. Each volunteer has a landline, a laptop, and stationary supplies. My small office is off the main room. Lucy, our manager, has an adjoining office, though she spends all her time with the volunteers.

Lucy is amazing. A lovely lady from the Dominican Republic, with such a kind face. She speaks Spanish and Creole and used to be a paralegal until she started to agree with all the jokes about lawyers.

The first group of Help Center volunteers are standing around, chatting and sipping coffee, or trying out their computers with Lucy's assistance. Eight women and two men are here. I've already met them and thanked them profusely for coming. Now, as we walk in, they all stare at Nick. I introduce him and they clap.

"Nick is going to be advising us about the legal rights of people who call in with complaints," I explain. "All the people who call in, not only the ones we put on the news. And to get ready, he's agreed to give us a few lectures."

"Talks, not lectures." Nick smiles.

"Talks about consumer law. Ask him any questions you have. I have a boatload of questions, so we'll all learn together."

"Nick, are you going to be on TV?" This from Matthew: a slender man in a Key West t-shirt.

His friend Alex grins.

"Yes, he will," Bob, the news director answers.

I didn't notice he'd slipped in behind us.

"Nick's from around here," Bob says, "and he was assigned to us by the attorney general himself, Leland Davis. So you can see that everyone takes this seriously."

"We're still going to have fun, though," I add, because at a weathered six-foot-four, Bob Beardsley can be a little intimidating. "Especially once you've gotten into a rhythm."

"Oh, I'm going to tell you about rhythm," a lady says, from the back.

Not knowing how to respond, I ask, "Is Lucy, who's wonderful—"

"Yes, she is," everyone concurs.

"Is she making everything clear for you? The phones and the computers and everything?"

"You can say goodbye to Lucy," the same lady says, in a broad Cuban accent.

She's about sixty, with a gold bouffant, a purple-striped sleeveless top, short white skirt, and sky-high red platforms.

"I'm taking Lucy home," she announces. "When my husband meets her, he'll finally leave me and I'll be free to go dancing."

Lucy belly laughs. "Lizzie, Nick, this is Alicia Balart."

"The *real* Alicia Balart," the lady proclaims. "Not that skinny Minnie you see on television."

"Alicia," Lucy says, "is our Alicia's aunt."

"Alicia is my *niece*. She was my niece a long time before anyone called me her aunt. But go ahead, call me Aunt Alicia. I wasn't blessed with children of my own, so I have three nieces named Alicia. Not in the same family. My sister and two brothers each named their daughters Alicia, because they know what's good for them. And I have three nephews. Al-fonso, Al-varo, and the last one is plain Al."

When we all stop laughing, I prompt, "Your niece says you already have a story for us, Aunt Alicia."

"I do. Put down the phones. We don't need nobody calling in."

"It's about your landlord?" I ask.

"That lousy *rrrrr-ata*! We've got to expose that louse and get back my cable TV. How am I supposed to watch you? But that's not the story. Not the *first* story."

"What's the first story?" Lucy asks.

Nick is buttoning up a guffaw.

"I told you. Dancing." Aunt Alicia swings her ample hips. "It's not my problem. My Carlos didn't let me cha-cha-cha with this *jamonero*."

"What's that?" Nick asks.

"What's that?" Aunt Alicia racks her brain and makes a face. "A guy who always wants to touch you. Not to dance. This guy, this oily dance instructor, took three of my girlfriends—widows who don't have a Carlos to look out for them—and he... emptied their bank accounts. They'll talk in front of the camera. Except maybe Harriet. She still has a thing for this mambo king."

"Great," I say. "I mean that's terrible, but we'll investigate."

"Meantime," Aunt Alicia asks Nick, "how do you like my shoes?"

"Stunning."

"He don't say a lot, but I like him. And I like your tie. However," Aunt Alicia pulls the bow and the tie comes undone, "*this* is the way you want to wear it. To look sharp. Let it down. And undo your shirt button. Do it."

Nick does.

Alicia stretches her arms. "Yes? Yes?" she asks the room.

Lucy, Bob, and the volunteers whistle and applaud.

7

LIZZIE

"Want to grab some lunch?" Nick asks.

This catches me off guard. After we left the Help Center, he pretty much said nothing. *"Nice space. Lucy's great."* That's about it. Now we're in the lobby. I should've guessed he was feeling wild and crazy. The bowtie is still dangling and he's holding his jacket draped over his shoulder like some nerdy member of the Rat Pack. He seems capable of anything. Maybe even conversation.

Nevertheless, "I really have to get back to the Help Center."

"Lucy's there."

"Look—"

"Don't you think we ought to get to know each other? A little?" He's not asking. It's more like a challenge.

"Are you still trying to get out of working with us? Because if you are, this is pointless."

"I'm not."

I stare at him, which isn't hard. "What changed your mind?"

"Alicia."

"The aunt?"

"Both of them. All of them."

I don't smile. I refuse to smile. He really was a jerk on the phone. Still.

"I'll have to go back for my purse."

"Lunch is on me. And my car's right across the street. You know, our office—"

"Yes, I know. I looked you up. I know everything about you."

Nick seems more embarrassed than I expected.

"That's how I know you dated Karen."

He smiles. "Do you know my favorite Disney movie?"

I consider. *"Beauty and the Beast.* You can relate."

"Nope."

"Then, which?"

"You'll have to come to lunch to find out."

I tell Arlene at the desk that we're going, and ask her to tell Lucy. Our volunteers will be all aflutter. The women were swooning over Nick. The guys, too.

We cross the street and ride the elevator in his building down to the garage. He beeps a distant car.

When I see it, I can only shake my head. "Austin Powers lent you his ride?"

Nick holds the door open for me. Sometimes I resent that, along with pulling out chairs. My dad never did chivalrous stuff like that that for my mom. Although, I think sometimes she wanted him to, especially when they were out with company or the in-laws. But honestly, it's never come up with most of the guys I know.

I climb in. The top's already down. I worry that my hair's going to blow out like Bridget Jones in the convertible with Hugh Grant. And stay that way, like Albert Einstein.

"Where are we going?" I'm hoping it's not on the highway. I don't even have a brush.

"What would you say to the Biltmore? We could eat outside, by the pool."

"Okay."

Okay? I've *always* wanted to eat at the Biltmore, but no one's ever wanted to go. This is the most luxurious hotel you've ever seen. It's about a hundred years old and looks like a Moorish castle. Lush gardens, gushing fountains, tiled courtyards and colonnades. I shot a story once in the lobby. The ceiling is right out of a medieval manuscript, a blue night sky spangled with gold stars. I still have the picture on my phone. Looking at it makes me happy, knowing something this beautiful is so near.

Best of all, the Biltmore's in Coral Gables, a ritzy community south of Miami. No highway. So I won't arrive with what looks like a fright wig.

Nick valets his Jaguar. We take in the lobby and then walk out to the pool. Oh, my. This is right out of golden age Hollywood. Enormous. Elegant. And ringed by tables with umbrellas, where the host seats us. I'm so delighted, I smile at Nicholas. Right now, calling him Nicholas is almost an endearment.

"If you like this," he grins, sensing my joy, "maybe you'll let me take you sometime for Sunday brunch in the courtyard. I'll show you on the way out."

It would be rude to ask if he's putting this on his expense account. And glancing at the menu, I see it's actually not as expensive as I figured. Why haven't Meg and Ardis and I ever come here? Well, I'm here now and I'm going to be pleasant.

"So why didn't you tell me you went out with my sister?"

Crap. Blurted that out, so I bury my head in the menu.

***

NICK

Why didn't I tell her?

Going out with Karen Lomax is nothing to be ashamed of. A lot of men would boast about it. And it's not as though I'd forgotten about her. You see Karen on TV. You see her on magazine covers. And now, sitting here in this beautiful hotel, I remember another hotel, the Hermitage in Nashville, and the last time Karen kissed me.

She joined a sorority at Vanderbilt, and although the girls seemed sweet, Karen wasn't really close to any of them, including the handful that Vandy allowed to live in the house with her. In all the time we went out, we never double-dated or even went to a sorority party.

For some people, the high point of life is high school. That's not a knock. Often, it means they've kept friends since kindergarten and everything comes together when they're teens—sports, theater, maybe even the girl or guy they wind up marrying. For other people, the high point is college. Their first taste of freedom. The first time you feel smart or talented or attractive. The first time you fit in, even if only with a small circle of quirky friends who haven't known you your whole life and don't expect you to live down to their expectations. Who instead allow you to reinvent yourself.

Then there are people like Karen. High school and college and their first jobs are all stepping-stones toward a prize that's always kept within sight. If they're truly smart, they don't put on blinders, they enjoy each step along the way. But I'm not sure Karen did. She wasn't cloistered. I was one of a whole line of guys she went out with, though I gather she was always monogamous. Serially monogamous. And there were times when sleek, accomplished, driven Karen Lomax made me feel I was the one.

When I met her, she was sitting next to a big naked guy lying on his back. Okay, the guy was naked because he was the Greek god of wine, a copy of a statue from the Parthenon in Athens. Back in the 1890s, for the hundredth anniversary of Tennessee statehood, Nashville held an exposition and built a full-scale replica of the most famous temple in ancient Greece. Our Parthenon is in a park across from campus, and at night they light up each one of the dozens of columns. And even if you're no classical scholar, which I'm not, it's mysterious and thrilling to see this glorious temple aglow in the dark. I often went there to study. That's what Karen was doing, too, on that late Tuesday afternoon in March when there were few tourists and no other visitors and we had the place almost entirely to ourselves.

"Sorry," I said, or probably stammered. "Didn't mean to disturb you."

"Thank you," she said without looking up.

"It's just that I normally sit here. On this bench. To study."

Now she did look up. And her look was withering.

"Then I guess I'm the one who's sorry," Karen said, in tones much more clipped than the lingering way most people speak down South. "When I asked Dionysus here if this seat was taken, he said no."

"And did he offer to buy you a drink?"

She ignored me and went back to her book written in an alphabet I didn't recognize.

Vanderbilt can be somewhat formal, even for a Southern school. That's one reason I liked it. Students still dressed for football games like they were going to a garden party. But they looked like gardeners compared to Karen. Instead of slumping over a notebook and noshing a bag of chips, she sat there regal and unruffled and downright dismissive.

I took the bench on the opposite wall and pretended to look at my book. She wasn't fooled. I guess she was used to it. Finally, at closing time, before the guards could kick us out, Karen rose and I did, too. She smoothed her blue pleated skirt, gathered up her things and looked me straight in the eye.

"What are you studying?" she asked. "Or should I say, not studying."

"Pre-law. Econ and history."

Karen nodded, knowingly. "A future master of the universe. Like your father?"

So she knew. He'd been all over the papers, all over the country. Not because of who he was. My father was another rich bastard. But the company he kept—and the entertainment he provided for them—made headlines and also shone a small spotlight on me here in Nashville and no doubt back in Miami, as I'd find out after graduation. In the meantime, I ignored Karen's question.

"My mother is a judge," I told her, and left it at that.

We walked out together. It was now twilight and I was in the clouds on Mount Olympus, until Karen stumbled on one of the stone steps. She didn't fall. I caught her. But her furious flash of, "Dammit," was loud enough to draw out a guard.

Wayne knew me because I came so often, so I felt humiliated when he yelled, "What the hell are you doing to her?"

"Nothing. Nothing," Karen said, still overwrought.

Wayne stood by, outside the huge bronze doors, watching us leave. Perhaps to reassure him—certainly not because she felt some sudden rush of affection—Karen took my hand, and we strolled back toward campus. She'd hurt her ankle but refused to wince, much less limp. When I asked if I could call a cab, she shook her head, so I said nothing else, almost giddy we were still holding hands.

Believe it or not, from there things moved pretty quickly. I'm still not sure why. We went to baseball games, movies—Karen loved *Slumdog Millionaire* and talked of wanting to work in India. After seeing that film, I thought she was nuts. She thought I was nuts taking her to the Grand Ole Opry. Trust me, it's no ramshackle barn. The new place is as grand as New York's Metropolitan Opry. Country's not my favorite music. I like jazz. But Alan Jackson was great, especially singing the nostalgic ballad, "Remember When." I admitted trying to write ballads myself.

"You write songs?" Karen asked, surprised.

I rarely surprised her.

"Yes, ma'am."

"Sing one," she ordered.

"I can't sing."

"Not even to me?" she said, in a sing-song Southern accent.

"Not even in the shower. When I try," and I started to yodel, *the hot water turns cold and I slip on the soap.*"

She didn't laugh. Karen almost never laughed. Or I wasn't that funny. We were walking from the show to the Opryland Hotel for a drink by the indoor waterfall that's as lush as Tahiti.

Karen asked seriously, "Then what's the point of writing songs?"

"Actually, I have an old friend, Harry Mattis, back in Miami. He's a giant. Nearly seven-feet tall. But Harry's got a tenor voice that you'd swear sounds like Alan Jackson's."

"And he sings your songs? Where?"

"Some small clubs back home."

I hadn't yet asked Karen to visit Miami. We hadn't gotten that far.

"And is that what you really want to do? Write songs?"

A month into our relationship, what I did, or didn't, really want to do had become a familiar refrain. Karen sensed I lacked the passion to become a high-powered attorney. She sensed that, because she was passionate about her own future. It was all mapped out. By senior year of college, Karen wanted to use her language skills to become a foreign correspondent. Christiane Amanpour was her role model. They'd met at a UN function in New York. Amanpour was the one who suggested Karen spend a post-graduate year at Oxford to improve her Arabic.

My own path was respectable enough, and one for which anyone would be grateful. By that March, I knew I'd be attending Yale Law School. But Karen knew that was the next conventionally successful thing to do, the next turn of the merry-go-round. You know who should've been my role model? Harry. Like me, his parents went through an ugly divorce when we were kids. Unlike me, Harry is black and that made life tough in Miami, where the pecking order for too many people is white, then fair-skinned Cuban, then other fair-skinned Latinos, then dark-skinned Cuban, dark-skinned Latino, African American, and then Haitian. Bucking stereotypes, Harry had studied criminology at the University of Miami but was skipping grad school to enlist in the Marines. He had wanted me to join him. Yet even knowing a few years of serving my country and marching out of my comfort zone was the right thing to do, I lacked the guts to hop off that carousel.

My last date with Karen was supposed to be spectacular. I was trying to wow her. On that May weekend before graduation, I asked her to wear something formal and bring an overnight bag. This wasn't a shocking proposition. We'd been intimate for a while, but Karen disliked staying at the house five friends and I rented, although David, my roommate, never gave us a hard time about having to sleep elsewhere. Unlike Karen's roommate, who was clearly jealous, and not of me. Also, Karen found nothing seductive about my waterbed.

I picked her up at the Theta house, while the other girls peeked through the curtains. Although I had a car, we took a horse-drawn carriage to the Parthenon. It was closed by then, so we sipped champagne on the steps. Not the one she'd tripped on. Then the carriage took us downtown to the Hermitage Hotel, dedicated to *belle époque* grandeur, the lobby all marble, with a soaring painted glass skylight. We checked in and dined at the hotel's Capital Grille.

Having gone vegan after *Slumdog*, Karen didn't sink her teeth into a steak, but the evening was still sizzling when we got back to our room. Until about three in the morning, when Karen's cell rang. It was her sister. Up 'til then, I didn't know she had a sister. Karen called her Lizzie. Their father had been shot, He was in a hospital in Cincinnati, in the ICU. Karen said she'd be there in four hours or less.

"I'll drive you," I said.

"No, I've got to go."

She had a car, too, an old Miata back at Theta.

"You're exhausted," I said. "And all keyed up."

"It's okay." Karen changed into the shorts and top she'd packed. She seemed calm but kept fumbling with her blouse buttons.

"How was your dad shot? Why?"

"He was… at work." Now she was getting tense.

"Work? What kind of work?"

Karen had never told me. As I had never discussed my father.

She stopped and drew a breath. "My father is a police officer. A Cincinnati police officer. And my sister—"

"Lizzie?"

"My sister says he was patrolling in a bad neighborhood and got shot. All right? Can I finish getting dressed now and go?"

"Let me help you with that button."

"What?"

"I can—"

"Please." She pushed away my hand and stuffed her dress and heels into her bag, then left.

And that was it. Karen ignored my calls. Her sorority sisters said they didn't know why. I considered driving up to Cincinnati, having gotten the Lomax's address from a friend at admissions, and then realized that would only make things worse. What things? I didn't know.

Barbara, one of the Theta girls, later told me Karen skipped graduation even though her father was recovering. My mother came with my Aunt Sue. They stayed at the Hermitage.

I kept track of Karen from afar. She was off to Oxford, then Houston, then I watched her reporting from Iraq, and then I saw her everywhere—on TV and in the tabloids with a lot of guys, from Josh Hutcherson, who's much shorter than Karen, to Kwami Thomas, who's much taller.

So now, sitting with her sister across the table at a hotel as nice as the Hermitage, why hadn't I told Lizzie right away that I'd gone out with Karen?

"It didn't seem important," I lie.

***

LIZZIE

I know he's lying because his head is buried in the menu. I let the conversation about Karen drop. God knows what I'll blurt out if we order a drink.

"Hello, my name is Bernard. What can I bring you to drink?"

"Lizzie?" Nick asks.

"Water for me, please." Not taking any chances. "And may I have a lemon?"

"Of course." Bernard winks.

He's probably being friendly, but I want to tell him that I don't plan on adding sugar to make lemonade, as I often do. The Biltmore is too grand for that.

Nick orders raspberry iced tea.

"What do you drink when you're drinking?" I ask.

"The same. I really like iced tea or Arnold Palmers."

"Are you a fitness nut?" Blurted that out, too.

Oh, this is going well.

"Yeah. Apart from the occasional hot fudge sundae. And pizza. And of course, Oreo cheesecake from Fireman Derek's. Have you been there?"

"No."

"I'll take you."

When? *Did I say that out loud? No, thank goodness.*

Nick orders a grilled chicken salad. I order a burger. It's worthy of the setting. He and I haven't talked about anything but the hotel and Coral Gables and why they built this hotel in the middle of Coral Gables instead of by the ocean. We don't know. Maybe I'll ask Bernard so I can hear his charming European accent again.

Meantime, I ask Nicholas, "Why were you such a creep on the phone?"

"What?"

"I'm sorry. But why were you so pompous? Dismissive? Arro—"

"Because I was a creep," he admits.

"Why? Now you seem nice. And you seem happier without your tie and jacket. Were you wearing a tie and jacket when I called?"

"Yes."

"So what does this tell you, Nicholas? When I spoke to Karen—"

Aarggh. Why am I bringing up Karen? What do they put in this water?

Oh well, soldiering on. "Karen says you were formal, even back in college. And that your father—"

***

<u>NICK</u>

I don't want to talk about my father, so I go on the offensive.

"Do you do everything your sister does?"

Dammit, now she's hurt.

"I'm sorry."

She says nothing. We eat.

"I really am sorry, Lizzie."

"No, it's a reasonable question." She's now distant. "I don't do everything my sister does. I'm not able to. I didn't get into Vanderbilt. I don't speak any foreign languages. And WTAN's Help Center is not *Backstory*."

"You're one of the best reporters I've seen anywhere. You're the reason I want to help. I've seen how you take a two-bit feature story—"

"The kind we do on local TV."

"Please, let me get this out."

"Because who knows when you'll open up again."

"Lizzie, you turn ordinary stories into something special. And I really do think we can do some extraordinary stories and make them great."

"All because you met Alicia's aunt? Or is this an apology?"

"Both. And it's true."

We eat some more. Lizzie doesn't talk to me. She does ask Bernard why the Biltmore isn't on the ocean, like the Breakers up in Palm Beach. Bernard has no idea and instead notes that his hotel does have an excellent golf course. Have we offended Bernard? No. He doesn't seem to have as much invested in the Biltmore as Lizzie does. I saw the way she looked at that ceiling, like it was the enchanted one in Harry Potter.

"What's your real name?" I ask.

"What?"

"Your real first name. Elizabeth?"

"Yeah."

I think about this. Elizabeth, Lizzie. "From Jane Austen."

"*Pride and Prejudice*. My mother's a high school English teacher."

"Karen isn't from Jane Austen."

"My aunt's name is Karen."

"Like Alicia."

"But in our generation, there's only one Karen," Lizzie says. Changing the subject she points out, "Your mother is a judge."

"Right."

"I read that. What does your father do?"

I say nothing. Then, "He's out of the picture."

***

LIZZIE

Clearly Nick doesn't want to discuss this, so I let it drop even though it's bothering me.

Bernard offers to bring the dessert cart. I'm dying to see it but say no. Nick asks if I'm sure. I'm not at all sure but insist that I am, and Nick says maybe next time, when we come for brunch. Okay. I have something to dream about.

He pays and we watch little kids splashing in the pool. Which looks like something a Roman emperor might've waded in on the Isle of Capri, complete with an endless colonnade and statues of goddesses. Do these children think a place like this is normal? I was lucky growing up. We weren't rich, but everyone in my neighborhood lived more or less the same, and it was enough. Plenty.

I tell Nick, "You didn't ask about *my* father. He's a cop."

"Yes, I remember Karen saying that. He was wounded when we were in college."

"He was." I think about that and remember.

Dad was chasing an armed robbery suspect down an alley at 2 a.m. The guy shot my father in the chest. Dad survived, but it was a near thing. I was a freshman studying broadcasting at the University of Cincinnati, so Mom and I got to the emergency room right away. Karen rushed home from Nashville.

"Is he doing okay now?"

"Oh, yeah. They put him on desk duty, but he's back on the job." I laugh. "Except when he's home watching Hallmark movies."

"What?"

"Those romance movies on the Hallmark Channel."

"He and your mom must have a happy marriage if he enjoys watching that kind of thing."

"Oh, Mom doesn't watch with him. She likes action movies, like *The Avengers*. So much for Jane Austen. Today, she might've named me Black Widow. But yes, they have a happy marriage. Two people don't have to be the same."

We watch the kids swim a little more, then stroll through the starry lobby to look over a balcony at the courtyard. If we ever do go back, it'll be a magical place for brunch.

"Wait." I grab Nick's elbow. "You said if I ate with you, you'd tell me your favorite Disney movie."

"*Lady and the Tramp*. I never had a dog. But I love meatballs."

8

LIZZIE

"The Biltmore. What were you wearing?" Karen asks.

"You know the green that's kind of ruched?"

"You look great in that. It brings out your eyes." My sister teases, "Were you trying to dazzle him?"

"I was trying to eat a burger without getting it on my dress."

"That's not enticing."

"No, it's not. This was a get-acquainted work lunch, Kary."

"Okay."

"And you don't care about Nick," I ask, "do you?"

"Desperately."

We're not Skyping or FaceTiming, so I can't see her face.

I change the subject, sort of. "No chance you're getting back with Kwami?"

"We've moved on."

"To what? Or who. Whom."

"To whom?" Karen laughs. "Is this call being edited?"

I laugh, too. "Are you already seeing someone else?"

"Not really. Kwami is. Didn't you see?"

"No."

"Vanessa J."

"That could be tabloid garbage." I scoff. "Where did you see that?"

"Everywhere. Catch up on your gossip and stop mooning over Nick Harris."

I don't protest. Is Kary wondering why I don't protest? Mooning over Nick is a bit strong. I find plenty of guys attractive and some of them have taken more than a glance or two at me.

Growing up, I didn't date much. Our church was big into group dates, and—foreshadowing of future career, if only I'd known it—a local TV station did a story about the pledge our teen group took. We went roller-skating and bowling, to arcades and all kinds of other places as a group, eight or ten of us at a time. This was for high school sophomores and juniors. We told the reporter, Tricia Grundy, who was still at WXIK when I interned there, that group dating relieved us of a lot of pressure to get physical or too emotionally involved. We all said it and some of us believed it, including me.

Kary hadn't dated much. She was homecoming queen and got the leads in most of the school plays. We had the cast party for *Our Town* at our house, which was unusual because Kary didn't invite classmates over that often. Watching secretly from the staircase, I saw a few kids kissing on the basement sofa and one couple writhing around—fully clothed, but still—on the shag rug. This was before I knew what shagging meant. But Kary didn't do anything like that, not that I ever saw. The fact that she waited until college to date at all made me less eager to jump in.

When I enrolled at the University of Cincinnati, there was someone who seemed serious. I was a journalism major, minoring in film and media studies. This brought me into contact with students at UC's College Conservatory of Music. My mom, as an English teacher, steeped Kary and me in *Great Books*. Mom and Dad also took us often to Cincinnati's marvelous art museums. The big one has masterpieces from every period because Cincinnati was a leading nineteenth century city, Longfellow's Queen City of the West, and captains of industry donated their old masters and newer things as well.

One of the Cincinnati Art Museum's most haunting treasures is a Van Gogh showing a lonely couple in a menacing dense wood. Vincent painted that not long before he shot himself. My point is, we knew something about literature and art, but not music, classical music, even though Cincinnati has a fine reputation for that, too.

So I was moved to tears passing by a rehearsal room one day and hearing a string quartet playing what I later learned was Beethoven, and seeing the cellist looking like an angel. Not an angel. Angels are sexless. Rick Liebling was sexy as hell. I watched this bespectacled but virile blond guy straddle an instrument that looked like a woman's torso, and draw his bow, first gently and lyrically, then as madly as a lumberjack trying to saw his cello in half. When they finished, one of the two violinists facing the door where I was peering through a small window pointed me out to Rick, giggling. I ducked and ran. Rick opened the door and told me to wait. He was still holding his bow, and chuckling.

The upshot is we dated for the better part of a year. You know the jokes about band camp. Classical musicians are equally as horny. I lost my virginity. No lovely memories of that. Rick was virile and lyrical but not especially romantic except about music. Surprising still, how graceful he could be in his concert clothes, with the orchestra or his quartet, or playing Bach by himself, and then how grubby and smutty—that sounds prim, but there's no other word for it—when he was in a rutting mood with me. It hurt me to find that Rick didn't caress me the way he caressed his cello. He didn't cherish me the way he did a ravishing adagio by Mozart or Schubert. Instead, he had me pose for him in ways that feminists would say objectified me. But it was worse than that. Maybe that's why the way Harry Lutz was posing me hurt even more. Rick Liebling and Harry Lutz made me feel that I was not ravishing, merely serviceable.

So it was almost a relief when Rick told me that he'd be studying the next fall at the Mannes School of Music in New York. Immediately, I became an afterthought. By the time my father was shot that May, Rick didn't even call, although everyone at school knew. I didn't care. And didn't care about anyone else for a long while.

Changing the subject again with my sister I ask, "How's that explosive consumer story coming?"

"It's coming. You know, the producer does most of the set up. Lisa Nape. She's great. They want it for next month, so yeah, it better be coming."

November is one of the big sweeps months, when ratings count the most for advertisers. Even more for local news, but Kary doesn't ask me about the Help Center, which we're also pushing to get up and running for November.

Instead, she asks, "When's your next date with Nick?"

"Stop it. We've got a ton of work to do. If he doesn't hate me now, he's going to hate all the shoots. And all the work with the volunteers."

"Yeah, he's not great with people."

"They love him."

"Great. As long as you don't love him."

I laugh, but then ask, "Why not?"

"Well," my sister says, "he's still kind of mine, isn't he? I mean, wouldn't it be, I don't know—incestuous is putting it too strongly—but wrong to be with someone I was that close to?"

I've been lying on the sofa in my apartment, which doubles as my bed, but now I get up.

"You hardly mentioned Nick back in college. And when Dad was wounded, he didn't come. You didn't even want to take his calls."

Karen pauses. "It was an awful time. I didn't want to deal with boyfriends on top of everything else. But I did care about Nick Harris. I did."

"Do you still?" I ask again, wishing I hadn't.

"Of course. I care about everyone I let get that close. I mean, Lizzie, it's not like there have been that many. And I can't believe Nick hasn't asked about me."

"He did. In a joking sort of way."

"Well," my sister says, a little huffy, "I don't understand that. It was no joke. Not to me. Look," and now Karen's voice has gone up an octave and she's laughing a false laugh, "I've gotta go. *InStyle* is coming here for an interview."

"To your apartment? Have they seen it?"

"All straightened up. I used this as an excuse to call a decorator."

"One who cleans, I hope."

"*You,* stop it. The last time you were here, you're the one who left a mess. And Dad was impossible with that popcorn until Mom took it." Now Kary impersonates Mom, "I may fly down to Miami to see how *you* live, missy. Speak to you Sunday."

She smacks a kiss. I do, too. And then I have trouble sleeping.

9

NICK

"Is that supposed to be a cha-cha or a mambo?" I ask.

"Are you kidding?" Lizzie laughs. "She's lucky he's holding her up."

"Holding her up is right. As in, robbing her."

It's a week after our lunch and Lizzie and I are trying to nail down our first story after two of them fell through. Aunt Alicia was a lifesaver. All three widows, including Harriet Feinberg, agreed to be interviewed first by us, and then by State Attorney Ed Royce. Ed obtained a wiretap order based on their complaint and documentation. Bank statements show that Harriet is paying two hundred fifty dollars for this private dance lesson. The same rate Silvia Ramirez and Dotsie Klein are paying. The average price in Miami? Sixty bucks.

And who's the Fred Astaire worth four times more than his competition? In addition to the lavish lunches and dinners he cadges off clients, and—now we're talking felonies—the automatic deposits that funnel even more cash into his account?

Meet Jorge de la Cova. You're watching him right now through the plate glass window of his Miami Beach dance studio, while Lizzie and I loiter outside. Lizzie's miniature spy camera, attached to her purse, is recording video. A hidden microphone Harriet's wearing lets us hear them through wireless ear buds.

Harriet told us that Jorge is quite a handsome man. I think he looks like a rodent with dyed hair, white bell-bottoms, elevator shoes, and false teeth. Jorge and Harriet, who's at least eighty, are stepping and wiggling to a song called "Cherry Pink and Apple

Blossom White." And… can you hear that? Harriet, God bless her, is asking Jorge about the direct deposits.

"I was talking with Dotsie and Silvia…"

Step, step.

"and we were wondering…"

Cha-cha-cha.

"if it wouldn't be better, Jorge…"

Back, back.

"if we paid you by check. Or even cash."

Cha-cha-cha.

Jorge turns Harriet. We see them head on and in the mirrors that cover three walls. His brow is furrowed.

"Why a check, darling?" Jorge sounds wounded. "Isn't it simple now?"

"Yes, and I had no problem when you suggested these direct deposits…"

Cha-cha-cha.

"But, Jorge, we're all trying to get a better handle on our finances. We're going to a seminar at the Fontainebleau."

"Do you really want to worry your head about this?" Jorge presses his cheek to Harriet's. "I thought your husband set up everything so you have no worries."

Cha-cha-cha.

"I'm not worried, Jorge. But I told my daughter Melissa, who's a CPA—"

Jorge halts in mid-step. "You never told me about her. Melissa? Where does she work?"

"She has an office in New Jersey. Livingston. Melissa and her husband are coming down."

"When?"

"For Thanksgiving. And they want to ask you about our lessons. Meantime, she told me to pay you by check or cash. I'm happy to pay in cash, Jorge. And Melissa says you can give me a receipt."

They resume dancing. Then Jorge stops. This sudden starting and stopping is giving Harriet whiplash.

"Cash or check is fine," Jorge says, brightly. "And what's nice, darling, is that we're coming up on a discount. For the holiday."

"Halloween?" Harriet has a wicked sense of humor.

"No, the whole holiday season. All through Christmas, New Year's. I don't know, it may last forever for loyal students like you."

"How big a discount?" Harriet asks, innocently.

She ought to work for the AG.

"I think..." Jorge turns off the music, and in a tiny wheedling voice, asks, "I'd have to look, but I think... is seventy-five an hour okay?"

"From two-fifty down to seventy-five?" Harriet asks.

"Or even sixty-five. That's it. Sixty-five. A cash discount."

"I'm sorry I didn't pay cash before."

"Me, too." Jorge bares his teeth in what's not quite a smile. "But I'll make it up to you. You know I will, darling."

***

LIZZIE

Nick and I showed up for the last fifteen minutes of the dance lesson. I taped that with my spy cam, but Kevin Rafael, my favorite cameraman, is waiting across Collins Avenue. As arranged, Harriet asks Jorge to walk her to her car. We beat them to it. As Jorge opens the BMW's door for Harriet, we step into Kevin's frame.

"Mr. de la Cova?" I say.

"Yes."

"My name is Lizzie Lomax. I'm with WTAN's Help Center."

"What?"

"And this is Nick Harris."

Nick extends his hand. "How do you do? I'm an assistant attorney general."

"*What?*"

"And we'd like you to explain," I say, evenly, "why you're charging ladies like Mrs. Feinberg four times more for dance lessons than the going rate for instructors in Miami."

Harriet steps in front of the camera. "Plus free dinners. And you should see the way this man eats."

10

NICK

Back in the van, Kevin grins and gives Lizzie a high five. She's sitting in the passenger seat. I'm on a swivel seat in the back, next to a control panel. It's a live truck, but Lizzie's not going live with our story. She'll be putting together what they call a package, an edited story for our first Help Center spot next week, the first night of the November ratings book. I'm too far back in the truck for a high five. So I lean forward and brush Lizzie's arm.

In the Help Center, the volunteers greet us like conquering heroes. Lucy jumps up and down. Matthew and Alex run up and hug me.

Aunt Alicia grabs Lizzie and says, "Did I tell you? Did I tell you? I expect you to put me on television, sitting right in-between my niece and that *borracho*, John McIntyre. And they can tell everyone who pulled the pants down on that greaseball."

Aunt Alicia wants to dance. I gladly oblige.

Lucy promises to give the volunteers a sneak peek at the dance lesson. Then Lizzie has to log everything, meaning she has to view a download of what we shot, at the computer on her desk, and type time codes for the video and the audio—the sound bites—that she'll use in her script. When the script's approved by Bob Beardsley, the news director, Kevin will edit it.

Kevin and I had a chance to talk before we went out. His father plays jazz piano and Kevin's into jazz, too. He also loves the Miami Heat. So I've gotten to know Kevin a little, as well as Lucy, Aunt Alicia, and Matthew and Alex. But I haven't had one moment alone with Lizzie.

48

She offers to walk me out to the lobby. In the hallway, I meet the station manager for the first time. Doug Long apologizes for not having said hello before now. WTAN is owned and operated by UBN, and Long was at a corporate meeting in New York the first day I showed up. Friendly guy, and he seems excited about what we're doing, especially after Lizzie tells him how today went.

As we pass the makeup rooms, Alicia the anchor, pops her head out. She's wearing enormous curlers, only one of her eyes has mascara, and I'm thinking, well, it *is* almost Halloween. Except that Alicia is so lovely and effervescent that no one could ever call her scary. She takes full credit for introducing us to Aunt Alicia, who takes full credit for our story. But both of them are really happy for us.

On the way out, we have to pass through the studio. Lenny, the old floor director, wants to know how our first shoot went. I start to tell him, when Lizzie asks Lenny if we could have the studio to ourselves for a minute. He says sure and ducks out. Lizzie dims the lights. And before I can say anything, she kisses me. I put my arms on her shoulders. And then down her back. And then around her waist.

And finally, here I am kissing Lizzie Lomax and seeing all the stars on the ceiling of the Biltmore Hotel.

***

LIZZIE

I hope Lenny has plenty of halvah stashed away, because this kiss goes on for about half an hour. We may have to preempt the news it lasts so long.

When we finally come up for air, I flutter, "Why, Mr. Assistant Attorney General, I don't know what came over me."

"There's a line there about me coming over you as soon as you'll let me. But I'll skip that and say, Ms. Lomax, I have wanted to kiss you ever since you asked Jorge de la Cova why he charges so much for dance lessons."

"I have wanted to kiss you ever since that wonderful lunch, when you talked dirty about desserts."

"I wanted to kiss you even before we met. Ever since that Mother's Day story you did, with the old and the young mothers."

"I remember. Nicholas, you really are a softie."

"Is that okay?"

I kiss him again, softly. "Yes. I like soft fitness nuts."

Many kisses later, Lenny asks if he can come back in.

I call back, "No."

He comes back anyway. "That didn't take long."

Nick smiles. "Did you have a bet down, Lenny?"

"Of course. And these days, I only go for sure things."

11

LIZZIE

"Well, let's say the best since Arthur Greenwald," I say.

"Who's he?" Meghan asks.

"Guy I knew in sixth grade. We were playing spin the bottle. Do kids still play that?"

"No," Ardis deadpans. "Too much gender confusion."

They were asking if my kiss with Nick was the best ever. We kissed two hundred times before Lenny turned on the lights, but yes, each one was the best ever. By a long shot.

I'm back in our apartment, with Meg and Ardis. It's rare for us to be here together. Not because we don't love each other. We do. Even though we didn't know each other before a year and a half ago. That's when Ardis saw the place first and went to an agency to find roommates. I'd signed up with the same agency and raced to call her. WTAN had been located downtown, but I knew they were planning a move to Brickell. And this apartment is on Brickell, right down the street.

It's one of the avenue's older and slightly more rundown complexes. Still, three high-rise buildings, two giant pools, tennis courts, and a whole grove of palm trees. Not to mention a little grocery store exclusively for the tenants. Glam? Yes. And that's why it takes three of us to pay the rent. We may have to get three more roommates so we can eat.

Meg, Ardis, and I are sitting on our one nice piece of furniture, a navy blue L-shaped mid-century sectional. Ardis stretches out on the chaise lounge section, as usual. She did find the apartment. But that section belongs to me at night. The apartment has two bedrooms, one for Ardis and one for Meg. Because I come home so late, after our eleven o'clock news, I collapse on the sofa. It's not a sleeper, but I put on sheets. Meg has the biggest set of drawers and a good-sized closet. I keep my clothes there. The bathroom looks like a bomb went off at Sephora. God did not intend three women to share a bathroom.

We've angled the sofa a little oddly so we can all enjoy the glory of the apartment—a sliding glass door leading out to a balcony that looks onto Biscayne Bay. Sigh. There's a story that the writer Oscar Wilde sailed to America from England and told reporters he was disappointed by the Atlantic Ocean. Being from Cincinnati, where the only substantial body of water is the muddy Ohio River, I'm never disappointed by Biscayne Bay. In the morning, I don't mind when the girls wake me. I get to see the sun glinting on the bay's lazy waves. At night, it's the moon's turn. Sigh again. And soon I'm going to see it with Nick. Maybe.

Speaking of sailing, Meghan works on ships. She's an assistant cruise director for a large cruise line. As soon as we've saved enough and can coordinate our schedules, Ardis and I are taking a cruise to Bermuda. That's where her family's from. Ardis has a British, or I guess, Bermudian accent. Veddy posh. But she's trying to get her own clothing shop established. On South Beach, no less.

South Beach is the hot spot where they renovated all the old art deco hotels and bars, which spill onto the sidewalk leading to the sea. Driving the strip is like walking slowly through a museum. And I mean slowly. Crabs on the beach move faster than traffic on Ocean Drive. The buildings, with their killer rents, are sherbet—pink, green, and my favorite, coconut—and the girls and the guys wear as little as they can to cover up their thongs as they stroll or loll to blasting Latin beats. When they do need to dress, Ardis hopes they'll stop at her shop, Bermuda Blues. So apartment sharing—pardon me—flat sharing for Ardis is a must.

Meg could afford her own apartment, but being from Wisconsin, she's Midwestern practical like me. Since she spends more time on ships than as a landlubber, it makes sense to share. And she seems to like our company. We love hers. Meghan Walker is what my mom would call a sweetie. She has an adorable round face. Ardis Lightbourne is all sophisticated angles, like the sofa. She plays at being hardboiled, but she's a sweetie, too.

"When are you seeing him again?" Ardis asks.

"Again? I see him constantly. But it's all work. Besides that lunch at the Biltmore and the make-out session in the studio, we haven't been alone for five minutes. But we do have to eat. So is it okay if I invite him over for dinner Saturday night?"

"We're sailing Sunday morning," Meg says. "I can stay on board the night before."

"Thank you."

Now Meg and I look at Ardis.

"Saturday night, I'll certainly be out late. Crissie said there's a party at the Clevelander. Do you need me to kip—I mean, sleep at her place? Or wherever?"

"No. This would be dinner. Full stop."

"And cleaning up all night," Ardis says. "Remember the last time you tried to cook? And that was mostly takeout."

"Nicholas is helpful."

Meg asks, mischievously, "Even when he's not at the Help Center?"

"We'll see."

12

NICK

From Tuesday, when Lizzie asked me to her place for dinner, until that Saturday, life was a blur. The Help Center's not yet accepting calls. Lucy's spending the week coaching volunteers on how to summarize complaints and direct them to the right agencies. We need to make sure volunteers won't offer legal advice. However, we do want to help everyone we can. Lizzie and I plan to sift through all the call summaries to find the most interesting complaints—the ones the most viewers can relate to, or the ones that are most telegenic. We hope to find a good mix of practical, outrageous, and even hilarious stories.

Bob Beardsley, the news director, green-lighted Lizzie's script on the corrupt dance instructor and Kevin edited it. Meantime, we've shot three more stories. The Help Center is set to run twice a week and we want to get ahead of schedule.

The second story came from Frank Reedy, the station's maintenance manager. A custodian he knows slipped Frank surveillance video from a preschool in Aventura. You see teachers talking nonstop on their cell phones while little kids eat glue, tumble off tables, and yes, run with scissors. We confronted the owner, interviewed outraged parents, and then Lizzie asked me to do a standup, offering tips about choosing a safe preschool. Bob liked that and told me to include similar advice in all our stories.

The next story shows how a home security outfit wasn't monitoring as promised. The homeowners let Lizzie and me pretend to be burglars, and we could've stolen everything from jewelry to the dining room set, in full view of their security service's cameras.

The last story really got to me. A family in Overtown told Cheryl Nix, one of our volunteers, that people in the poorest neighborhood there are being overcharged for groceries—as much as forty percent more than they'd pay in places like Coral Gables or Coconut Grove.

The supermarket's local manager was sorry but blamed staggering levels of shoplifting and other crimes. He said that forces the chain to pay more for security and insurance, and that means customers have to pay more. He added that other stores have abandoned Overtown altogether, creating a food desert. My AG colleagues are checking out what looks like gouging.

But the real eye-opener was talking with the matriarch of that family, Ivy Lewis. This ninety-seven-year-old lady sat in her tiny home, under family photos and a plaque showing John F. Kennedy and Dr. Martin Luther King, Jr. She also showed us pictures of Overtown back when it was an officially segregated community. Miami's white founders, including my great-grandfather, called it Colored Town. Black people needed passes to go to neighborhoods like the Grove and Miami Beach.

"So we made do for ourselves," Mrs. Lewis told us, in a strong but quavering voice. "We had Booker T. Washington High School. We had libraries, our own grocery stores, and nightclubs. Sakes alive. White people from all over came to our nightclubs. And the colored entertainers who sang and danced at the big Miami Beach hotels, you know they weren't allowed to stay at those hotels. So Cab Calloway and Billie Holiday—you know who they were?"

"Yes," we said.

"And even Nat Cole. Nat King Cole. White folks loved Nat King Cole. Lamar," Mrs. Lewis said to her son, "what's that Christmas song Nat Cole sang?"

"The Christmas Song."

"Go on with your bad self." His mother slapped his arm and laughed.

"That's the title." Lamar began to sing, more like Barry White than Nat King Cole. *"Chestnuts roasting on an open fire..."*

"You can't go out your door at Christmastime without hearing that song, whatever it's called," Mrs. Lewis said. "But even Nat King Cole wasn't allowed to stay at the Miami Beach hotels. So luckily for him, we had the Mary Elizabeth Hotel. And they treated Nat—"

"Like a king," Lamar quipped.

His mother doubled over and slapped his arm again. "Go sit down somewhere. This is *my* TV story."

"So what happened to Overtown?" Lizzie asked.

Mrs. Lewis shook her head. "A lot of things. But I'll tell you one thing. How did you drive here?" She looked at Kevin behind his camera. "Did you do the driving?"

"Yes. On I-ninety-five," he said.

"I-ninety-five. Interstate ninety-five. You know where they ran I-ninety-five? Where they decided to build it? Right through the middle of Overtown. They tore down my sister's house, Aunt Esther's house, God rest her soul, so they could build I-ninety-five right through the heart of Overtown. And now here I am paying five dollars for a pound of chicken breasts."

"And that," Lamar said, "is highway robbery."

Soon after we shot that story, I received a voice message at my AG office. I wasn't going to mention this, and I haven't said anything to Lizzie because there doesn't seem to be any point, but it was from Karen Lomax. This was the first time in eight years that I'd heard from her. The first time since that night at the Hermitage Hotel in Nashville. I have no idea what she wanted because she didn't say and I didn't return the call. I'm sorry if that's rude, but if Karen has anything to say to me she can tell her sister. And I hope this isn't about her sister, because I can't imagine why Karen Lomax is suddenly interested in me.

***

LIZZIE

Preschoolers eat glue. It's a fact. You can't make this stuff up. And the calls from viewers haven't even started.

Promos are already running for the Help Center, but they don't include the phone number. That starts Monday morning. You don't see much of me in the promo and nothing of Nick, and that's fine. It's all the volunteers going through the motions of answering pretend calls. Mixed in is a montage of stuff Kevin's already shot—the dance lesson, the preschoolers, and Mrs. Lewis buying chicken. I lied to that lovely lady. Billie Holiday was only a name to me. But afterward, I pulled her up on YouTube and Lady Day is incredible. By the way, the promotions department didn't include Nick and me making like Bonnie and Clyde to show how that home had no security. And that's fine, too, because we look asinine.

So we have four stories in the can. The volunteers are raring to go. Harry Lutz, as you know, has already selected my debut dress, but I don't want to think about that. I want to think about Nicholas Harris, Esq., because any minute now, Tito at the front gate of my complex should be buzzing to find out if he can let Nick in.

He better.

13

NICK

This is a mistake. I don't mean seeing Lizzie. I've been aching to be alone with her all week. I mean arriving at her place with the wrong kind of gifts.

I was so touched when she offered to make us dinner. Then this other voicemail popped up on my office phone, from a British woman who sounded grim.

"Hi there. This is Ardis Lightbourne. You don't know me, unless you've been to my shop, Bermuda Blues on Ocean Drive. Probably not. Anyway, I'm Lizzie Lomax's flatmate, and I'm calling to save you from certain doom. Not so much you. I don't know you, and most people in government are villains. I want to save Lizzie from humiliation. She's lovely, and I don't mean just dishy, although that's likely all you care about. The point is that Lizzie Lomax can do many things brilliantly, but she cannot cook. The last time she tried, we had to scrape bangers off the ceiling. Sausages, to you. So do this. Bring her favorite food, hamburgers. Barbecue them on grills we have next to the bay. And do not tell Lizzie I said this, or I'll cut off your balls. Cheers."

I'm leaving my car in guest parking. Does Lizzie have a car? She walks to work. Seeing me teeter into her lobby with a racquet, flowers, groceries, and a duffle bag, the doorman offers to help. I thank him and say I've got it. This looks like a hotel lobby, with couches surrounding a small pool. Must be hell for parents and for the doorman. The pool is shallow, so I don't suppose it's a hazard, but… hey, idiot, loosen up. Not everything's an investigation.

Ardis Lightbourne and Lizzie are on the eleventh floor. Will Ardis be there? Hope not. Halfway down the fresh-smelling hall, I press the bell. Lizzie opens the door. She's wearing a white tennis skirt and a bright yellow top. She's radiant.

I call out, too loudly, "Hi. You look beautiful. These flowers match your outfit."

I brought sunflowers. Lizzie beams at them. Then her face clouds over. She sees the grocery bags. When Lizzie is suspicious or upset, her lovely brows lower and her luscious mouth compresses into a thin line.

"What's all this?" she asks.

"A surprise. I know how much you like burgers, so I brought some with all the fixin's. And cheesecake."

She looks at me. Hard. "You can be arrogant, Nicholas. And aloof. But I have never known you to lack manners. So what is this all about?"

"I thought—"

"Wait." Lizzie draws in a breath. "Did Ardis speak to you?"

"No."

"She didn't?"

"No."

Silence.

We're standing in the doorway. The groceries and the racquet and the bag with my other clothes are getting heavy.

"Ardis did not speak with me. She left a message."

Lizzie's lips disappear altogether.

Then she looks searchingly at the bags. "What kind of cheesecake?"

"Oreo. My favorite. Like I told you."

She steps back into the apartment and doesn't lock the door. I follow and gingerly place the bags onto the small round breakfast table in the kitchenette. A half-wall divides it from the living room, where they have a bigger table and a sectional sofa angled toward a sliding glass door. There's a hall to the right leading, I guess, to the bedrooms and bath.

I ask, "Can I put the flowers in water for you?"

"My cooking is not that bad."

I glance up at the ceiling.

Lizzie snaps, "Cut that out."

"All right, honey—"

"Don't you honey me." She points to the food. "This is rude."

"It is rude. I'm sorry. I'll never do anything like this again." I move to put my arms around her.

She flinches.

"Forget all this," I plead. "Freeze the burgers or give them away. Let's have what you're making. It's going to be delicious. What are you making?"

Lizzie mumbles something.

"I beg your pardon?"

"Salad."

And I see the ready-to-eat bags on the counter.

***

LIZZIE

Okay, I may not be Giada De Laurentiis or Rachael Ray, but I'm no fool. Yes, things didn't go well when Greg Hoard was here. He's the head of our sports department. We went on three dates, and dinner here was the last one. But nobody got hurt, and Ardis didn't have to do any cleaning. Meg and I did.

This all makes sense. Nick likes salad. That's what he ordered at the Biltmore, so that's what I got. I ordered a burger, so he brought burgers. And anyway, Ardis put him up to it, so we'll move on. Although, I seriously consider kicking Nick out and keeping the cheesecake.

"This is great." He's sitting on the sofa. "What a view."

"I thought you might like to play a couple sets of tennis and then jump in the pool before we eat."

He's surprised that I'm back to being so nice. I am nice. I could be a cruise director. This is some evening I've planned, right? Apart from the salad.

"Sounds wonderful. But could we add one item to the agenda." Nick pulls me in to kiss him.

"Hold on," I protest. "I'm forgiving, but I'm not easy. Unfortunately…" I kiss him and whisper, "you're irresistible."

"You didn't notice that five minutes ago."

"Nicholas, do you really want to go there?"

He kisses me so passionately I'm not sure I'm still wearing tennis shoes.

"No," he mutters.

We unpack the patties, buns, bacon, tomatoes, and three kinds of cheese. Plus lettuce, which I already had. I also have red wine for me, and raspberry iced tea for Nick. It'll all keep in the fridge. We have a cooler big enough to take most everything down to the grill.

We're both dressed for tennis, so that's first. On a Saturday night, the courts aren't busy and the pool and barbecue won't be either. People in our complex are mostly single or they have young children. There are a few elderly folks, like Mr. Falcone. He lives right across the hall. Meg and Ardis and I look in on him because he's the dearest man you've ever met. A widower. His son visits a lot, but we're his nearest family.

Coming out of the elevator as we're about to go down, Nick runs into our most notorious neighbor, Daniela Rojas. He tries not to stare. Although, I would understand. Daniela was Miss Colombia twenty years ago in the Miss Universe Pageant. She could be Miss Colombia today, even after having a daughter, Paola, who is now a freshman at the University of Miami. At sixteen. That's how smart she is, and as sweet as her mother, who's even sweeter than Mr. Falcone.

The only reason Daniela couldn't be Miss Colombia today is that she's no longer a miss. Her husband is Pablo Rojas, better known as *El Cocodrilo*. The Crocodile lives in Colorado, at the ADX Florence Supermax federal penitentiary, doing fifty years for heading a drug cartel. Daniela doesn't talk about him, but DeAndre, our doorman, says she and Paola visit. DeAndre also says we live in the safest building in Miami because nobody's going to mess with *Señora Cocodrilo*.

"Evening, Daniela," I say. "Can we give you a hand with that?"

She's been shopping, apparently for a hat. I'm surprised DeAndre didn't help carry her hatbox, but Daniela probably said she could handle it.

"No, thank you, *conejito*."

Daniela told me that means little rabbit. She thinks I work too hard. I don't.

"Shopping, I never need help with." She looks at Nick.

"Daniela, this is Nick Harris." I don't tell her he's with the AG's office, since that may seem sinister. "We work together."

"Always working. All hours of the day. And night. I hope you'll share some of the work so she can come home to us once in a while."

"I'll try." Nick smiles.

Who doesn't smile at Daniela?

"I hope you can watch us this Monday," I say. "The late news at eleven. We're doing our first Help Center story."

"Already? That was fast, to put it all together. I still want to come down and volunteer."

"Any time. Nick will help train you."

Daniela beams. There's everything friendly but nothing flirtatious about her. Probably to protect guys like Nick.

"I would like that," she says. "And, Lizzie, you know you don't have to tell me to watch. I watch every night, hoping to see you."

We kiss each other. Nick insists on holding Daniela's box while she retrieves her key. I'll tell him about Mr. Rojas later. But Nick won't be shocked. This is Miami.

***

NICK

"Forty-love."

That's Lizzie. Not crowing, merely keeping score. She's the one with forty.

Lizzie played tennis in high school and I did, too. Neither of us was good enough to make our college teams, but Lizzie says she plays most every morning with a young mother while her daughter takes swimming lessons.

I play evenings with a neighbor in my building who's going to be on the Help Center. That's not a conflict. Joel filed his complaint with our office a month ago. It's a problem that affects a lot of people in Florida. Joel saved up for years to buy a boat, a thirty-two-foot cabin cruiser. Since he's an optometrist, Joel and his wife, Shirley, christened it the *Eye-Eye*. The boat kept springing leaks, even after repeated repairs. And there were other problems. Neither the dealer nor the Italian builder gave satisfaction, so our story's looking into Florida and federal remedies for boats that are lemons.

I'm thinking of all this to keep from noticing how badly Lizzie's beating me. The second set should go better because I have more stamina. I run four miles every morning without fail, from my Miami Beach condo near 46th Street down to South Pointe Park and then back. So I've got Lizzie where I want her.

***

LIZZIE

Nick's good, but I'm better. He thinks I'm too short to have a killer serve. I'm not. And I have more stamina than he thinks. I'm actually easing up a little to keep it interesting. That sounds awful, but it's true. Dad always says it's harder to be a good winner than a good loser. So if my head swells up too much, I'll remember that I can't cook. As I'm sure Nicholas will remind me.

***

NICK

Well, I did get Lizzie where I want her. In a congratulatory hug that may get us arrested.

***

LIZZIE

On to swimming. I'm already wearing a suit under my skirt and top. We have showers by the pool and I brought towels, but Nick has to go upstairs to change. And this creates problems, because I have to keep him away from our bathroom.

I tried cleaning up. I really did. But unless we're going to have a garage sale, there's nowhere to put everything. Nick Harris's bathroom is no doubt better organized than Martha Stewart's, but I can't live that way. And even if I could, Ardis is a total slob, however elegant her diction. So I tell Nick we're having plumbing problems and ask him to use the bathroom in the lobby. Then, when he changes in Meg's room, which is neat, we can both shower by the pool. After we swim, he can shower outside again and then go back upstairs to change into a yachting outfit or whatever else he brought. I have a filmy yellow sundress. Yellow is a good color for me. I may even bring down the sunflowers.

***

NICK

I offer to take a look at her bathroom sink, but Lizzie says maintenance is on the way. Seems she has two roommates. Ardis, who's from Bermuda and who will be home late tonight, and Meghan, who works for a cruise line and is about to sail off. Judging from her room, Meghan runs a tight ship. On her dresser, she alternates family photos with souvenirs of her travels. My favorite is a carved wooden sea turtle. Lizzie says it's from Antigua. I've never been and neither has she.

***

LIZZIE

Oh. My. Goodness. The man may not play tennis like Roger Federer, but Nicholas Harris, Esq., deserves a spot in a Greek temple. Or Chippendales. Of course he's wearing plaid trunks instead of a Speedo. And he really slathers on sunscreen, I hope because he wants to rub me down next. But Nick looks like a Marvel superhero.

Is it shallow, or even sexist, to be going on like this? As we say at the Help Center, file a complaint.

***

NICK

Wow. Lizzie Lomax is the most beautiful woman I have ever seen. Alicia Balart already mentioned her legs. I'll say this, the rest of Lizzie lives up to the legs and then some.

***

LIZZIE

Go for broke. That's my philosophy, when it matters. Normally my bathing suits are pretty blah. For swimming laps, I wear a one-piece Speedo. Otherwise, a modest tankini. But for Nick, it was off to the Mermaids Boutique. As a child, I wanted to be the Little Mermaid, sometimes with legs, sometimes with a tail. The boutique had a white bikini with an off-the-shoulder ruffled top. Tasteful but tempting. And I'm happy to tell you, it has Nicholas drooling for the second time since I've known him. This time, over me.

***

NICK

Lizzie is more beautiful than her sister. And so much nicer. I'm going to make sure she knows it.

***

LIZZIE

I have sucked in my stomach long enough. Time for burgers. Nick changed back into shorts and a polo shirt. He looks good in anything. I'm in that yellow sundress, sitting next to my sunflowers at a picnic table by the bay. Our complex has three places to barbecue. This one is near the playset, but it's 8:30 and all the children are in. We have this glorious view of Key Biscayne all to ourselves.

Nick is flipping meat. He's seasoned it according to a recipe from a place called Louis' Lunch in New Haven, where all the Yalies go. Louis' claims to have invented the hamburger. I doubt that. Nick says they serve theirs on thin toast and the burger is so good they refuse to offer any condiments. My dad would say this proves everyone at Yale is a leftist dictator. I'm glad I went to the University of Cincinnati. While Nick honors Louis, I choose American cheese, bacon, and ketchup. Nick considerately brought it all, having watched me chow down at the Biltmore. As I said, couples don't have to be the same. And we're on our way to being a couple.

Then one thing on which we can agree, the *pièce de résistance*— the cheesecake. I may never wear a bikini again. And here I defer to

Nick, because while Cincinnati has a Cheesecake Factory, forgive me, this is better. This is the best.

***

NICK

The sun's down now. We're on a bench, trying to break the consecutive kisses record Lizzie and I set in the studio.

***

LIZZIE

Mmm. He gets points for quality as well as quantity.

***

NICK

Looking out at night on Biscayne Bay is better than what I see on Miami Beach. On the bay, you see the causeway and the lights of Key Biscayne. At night, my view of the Atlantic is nothing but black, unless you're actually on the beach, with the moon out, and you can wade a little into the waves. Lizzie and I will do that. We're going to do everything. I may even get her to try a Louis' burger with nothing but toast.

***

LIZZIE

I wish I could see Nick tomorrow.

***

NICK

I'd love to see Lizzie tomorrow. Trouble is, Mom's asked me to take her to Aunt Sue and Uncle Marty's for brunch. Which is no trouble, normally. I love them. Then I'm going with Harry, that friend since grade school, to see the Heat host the Knicks. It'll mean watching Kwami Thomas, who I read broke up with Karen. Is that why she called? She's desperate?

Look, I hope Karen's happy, because I sure am.

14

NICK

We're at American Airlines Arena for the Knicks–Heat game. The girl sitting next to me is having a ball. She's perhaps ten and her father's already bought her what the concession stand calls Chicken Ciao. It's the law—everything in Miami must have an exotic name. Chicken Ciao is good old chicken tenders served with waffle fries. But there's more. Next, Ava—I heard her dad call her that—wolfed down half of her dad's hot dog, a soft pretzel, and Sour Patch Kids candy. Somehow this skinny kid washed it all down with soda. All she needs now is a stomach pump. Lizzie could be pals with Ava. Although Lizzie, of course, would have included a hamburger.

Ava can thank my pal Harry Mattis for enjoying the basketball game, which a foul-mouthed fan's threatening to ruin. A client gave Harry a couple tickets, and he invited me. Harry's a partner in a security firm. Not the kind Lizzie and I investigated, where they didn't monitor their home alarms. Harry and his employees, men and women, provide muscle. He's one of the few people in the arena who could intimidate the players. That's no fun for people who have to sit behind my massive friend. All they see is the phone number for Semper Fi Security on the back of Harry's T-shirt. As I told you, he's a Marine, out two years, although leathernecks are never really out.

We met in third grade, when Harry's dad moved the family down here from New Jersey. Sonny Mattis has a big construction firm. They operate heavy equipment, including the giant cranes you see all over South Florida. Harry and his father get along pretty well, but Harry didn't want to go into the business with Sonny. Nepotism didn't appeal to him. Also, Mr. Mattis can be... let's say, overbearing.

He and Harry's mom divorced when we were sophomores in high school. That was a tough year for Harry. Major things, like the divorce. And little stuff, like not getting the part he wanted in *Oklahoma.* This sounds ridiculous, but it really stung.

You see, when we were twelve Harry had a growth spurt that was right out of *Jack and the Beanstalk.* In every direction. Overnight, he hit six-foot-two—Harry's now six-nine—and he packed on muscle the way they used to pack hides and supplies onto an ox. The thing is, Harry's always been incredibly good-natured and sensitive. Even though he could've flattened guys, Harry didn't want to play football because he doesn't enjoy contact sports. He does enjoy music. And with his fine tenor, Harry desperately wanted to be cast as Curly in *Oklahoma.* There was the chance to sing "Oh, What a Beautiful Morning." More important, we assumed gorgeous Heather Marciano would be playing Laurie. Think of all the time they could've cuddled while rehearsing "Surrey with the Fringe on Top." Instead, Mr. Hochberg cast Harry as Jud Fry, the hulking scary thug who tries to assault Laurie. Harry—always a team player, except with football and his dad's business—accepted the part. But I could tell he was miserable. Especially with all that was going on with his parents. The worst part was, Heather wound up going out with Todd Imbimba, who played Curly.

Anyway, after the University of Miami, Harry became a jarhead. He actually saw Karen Lomax doing a story in Iraq. He knew I'd dated her during college, but he was too shy to say hello. After retiring from active duty, Harry and a buddy from the Marines started Semper Fi. It's extremely successful and leaves Harry time to sing on the side.

Back at the game, Kwami drains a three-pointer from what seems like eighty-feet. The no-good Knicks are killing our guys. Kwami, of course, gets me thinking about Karen. But now, thinking about Karen gets me thinking about Lizzie.

"What are you grinning about?" Harry asks.

"Lizzie."

My friend grins, too. "I'm happy for you. Nervous about tomorrow?"

"I'm not on live. They taped my part. Do they still say taped?"

"I don't know. Ask Lizzie. I think everything's digital now. You know, anytime you want to share a meal, all three of us, I could bring Angie."

They work together. I don't think it's more than that. Harry's divorced more than a year from the sister of his Semper Fi partner, Max Wiley. As you can imagine, the marriage meltdown was ugly, but Harry and Max got through it. And now Harry's slowly wading back into the water. Before I can answer about Angie—

"Babbitt, you f***ing turd. Shoot the f***ing ball."

That's not Harry yelling, or me. The worst part of Dolphins, Marlins, and especially Heat games is fans lobbing F-bombs, louder and more obnoxiously as they guzzle more beer. The arena tries to police these schmucks. We still remember Jimmy Buffett getting tossed for cursing out a ref. And Jimmy's the Mayor of Margaritaville.

To muffle the four-letter barrage, Ava's dad covers her right ear and pulls her other one against his chest. Ava keeps eating. Harry shrugs and gets up to escort the Luke Babbitt fan out of the arena, by the scruff of his neck. That's not his job, but Harry thinks it is, what with a little girl there.

"I gotta go anyway," he says. "Good luck tomorrow, man. I'll be watching."

"Ooh-rah."

15

NICK

Within minutes of the number going up on the morning show, the Help Center phones start ringing off the hook.

Lucy scheduled only four volunteers to come in early. They were expected to stay three hours and then make way for the lunch shift. But consumer complaints pour in so fast and so steadily that Lucy asks Aunt Alicia, Alex, and Matthew to arrive early and stay late. Normally, the Help Center would remain open from ten 'til five, but these first couple days we want to take calls during the morning show. As many volunteers as can make it will be coming in tonight at ten. We'll party for an hour and then answer calls when our first story debuts on the eleven o'clock news.

We're set to run two new Help Center stories every week. The first, on Mondays at eleven. Then the same story will be repeated Tuesday during the morning show and again at five. Wednesday we'll have the next new story, repeated the same way on Thursday. Lizzie will appear live on set only at eleven and the next day at five, and that's a lot, with all the investigating and reporting we have to do. For now, Kevin Rafael's assigned to us and we're grateful.

I've played down the Help Center with Harry, not to mention Leland. But this really is exciting.

***

LIZZIE

I'm a total wreck. Nick and I are both answering phones. This won't be part of our normal job, because we'll be busy investigating, but there's no way the volunteers—who are so wonderful—can handle this truckload of calls. And good calls, too. Many of them heartbreaking. But we're going to help.

Just as well that I've had this distraction all day. Because otherwise, I'd be depressed about the dress. Who had the nerve to call it a dress? This thing is short enough to qualify as a blouse. Once again Bob went to bat for me, but the network thinks Harry Lutz walks on water. Oh, well. It's not like I'm dancing on tables. I'll just be sitting on one.

***

NICK

After all the work and anticipation, I'm not sure our story's going to squeeze into the show tonight. A tropical storm is battering Cuba. The computer models, as usual, are all over the place, and usually wrong. This storm may not even strengthen. I hope not, for Lizzie's sake, the volunteers', and mine.

***

LIZZIE

Cris and Valerie have been cutting into programming all night. Cris Robinson is our chief meteorologist. Valerie Apuzzo normally works mornings. I was afraid Lutz would blow air up Valerie's skirt to show how high the winds are. But this is serious, and I marvel—we all do—at how calm and professional Cris and Val are when South Florida has to be talked off a ledge.

It's now 10:45, and Bob is telling me to get ready. Weather will be taking up the first block of the show, but it's holding off enough for sports and the Help Center to sneak in later. Alicia wishes me luck. Greg Hoard, the sports guy, plants a kiss and gives me a high-five. We did go out three times, so it's not harassment. And he's not a bad guy. Still, I'm glad Nick's in the Help Center, getting ready to take calls.

Our opening graphics normally feature John, Alicia, Cris, and Greg, with a montage of skyline and beach beauty shots. But because of the storm, we open with a special weather alert. Cris and

Val appear right off the top. They don't take the WE'RE-ALL-GOING-TO-DIE approach of at least one competitor, which shall go nameless, though everyone in Miami knows the station I mean. If it drizzles, those other guys tell viewers to start building Noah's ark.

We're at the first break. I go to the anchor desk. The prompter has my scripted open, but I'll be chatting with Alicia before that about what the Help Center's all about. John gives me a thumbs-up. Lenny brings the wooden block Alicia uses when she has to stand next to John. I step onto it to climb on the desk. And we're off. The Help Center logo and phone number are lighting up all three of the huge video screens. The control room punches up John's camera.

He reads, "*A boat that won't float? A supermarket charging forty percent more than other stores a few miles away? And a dance instructor who appears to be taking all the wrong steps. Tonight's the debut of our new consumer Help Center, where you can call for help... right now!*"

The control room switches to a medium shot of Alicia standing next to me, on a riser. You see us both waist up.

Alicia says, "Heading the new Help Center, our own Lizzie Lomax. She's working with volunteers you can see right now."

Harry Lutz told the whole newsroom to say *right now* and *breaking news* at least fifty times a show.

We switch to a live shot of the Help Center. Wow, the room's filled with volunteers, including Nick, answering calls or at least looking like they are. Hope they had a nice party and didn't drink too much.

Alicia says, "And Lizzie, our Help Center has quite an important partner."

"Yes indeed, Alicia. Florida's Attorney General, Leland Davis, has assigned us a deputy, Nick Harris."

Kevin zooms in to a tight shot. Hope Nick doesn't mind that I called him deputy instead of assistant. It sounds better, and anyway, we give his full title during Nick's standup in the package.

"Now you're about to see us in action," I say.

The shot switches again. Now it's me lounging, full-length, on top of the anchor desk with my legs crossed.

"We're taking you to Miami Beach, a dance studio where a lovely lady and her friends learn a hard lesson"—pregnant TV pause—"about more than dancing."

Dave Ashbrock, the control room director, plays our package. It begins with Harriet and Jorge clomping along to "Cherry Pink and Apple Blossom White." We hear from Dotsie and Silvia about the direct deposits. You see how Jorge's prices way exceed the average in Miami. Nick, who photographs even better than he looks, explains which laws may've been broken and how to protect yourself. And then the climax—Nick and I confront Jorge outside his studio. Jorge screeching, "Whaaat?" is priceless. Kevin freezes his face and edits in the last three notes of that *cha-cha-cha.*

Now we're live back in the studio, an even wider shot of me on the desk, legs dangling, skirt riding up to my armpits. I chat briefly with Alicia and John sitting behind the desk. They show the Help Center phone number on the big screens and we now see the volunteers and Nick answering a ton of real calls. We end with Alicia teasing Wednesday's story, the one about Mrs. Lewis's chicken.

<u>16</u>

LIZZIE

Everyone in the studio congratulates me. We have only a minute before Cris's next weather hit, followed by sports. So Lenny, who's faster than you'd believe possible at his age—faster than most of the dogs he bets on—slides over Alicia's wooden block. Awkwardly, I dismount from the desk, and this time there's no doubt I've made a spectacle of myself, as confirmed by a cheer from the floor crew. Anticipating that, I wore my granny panties. They all find this funny.

I try to smile and head over to the Help Center. No time for congratulations there. I grab a phone and answer a question about how to change an air conditioner filter. Turns out, most of the calls are like that, people needing help with what seem to be little problems until they happen to you. We're caring, and I hope, helpful to everyone. That's the first thing Lucy drilled into our heads, even Nick's. And for every twenty calls, there's at least one we want to put on the air.

***

<u>NICK</u>

Callers didn't really stampede us 'til after our story aired. So we had a chance to watch Lizzie on the Help Center's TV set. She sounded both tough and warm. And my girlfriend looked hot, almost embarrassingly so. Well, I guess this is show business as well as journalism. Lizzie hasn't talked much about the guy who forced her to wear that dress, but I know her well enough by now to see that she's throwing herself into work because she's understandably upset.

***

LIZZIE

Mom and Dad are calling my cell phone. They could watch on their desktop because our station live-streams.

"That dance instructor was so slimy I expected the woman to slip out of his arms." Dad laughs.

"Great story," Mom says. "Great job. And you were beautiful."

"But why did they make you look like you work at a strip club?" Dad wants to know.

"Dan," Mom warns.

"Okay. But it seemed—not you, honey, but that outfit—unprofessional."

We say goodbye. They promise to watch on Wednesday. Big kisses.

It's now nearly midnight. These magnificent volunteers—I haven't mentioned Diana Hopkins, who's in a wheelchair because of MS, or Peggy Chang, or so many others—Lucy is shooing them all away and thanking five of them in advance for coming in for the early shift tomorrow. Wonderful people. They deserved more than to have me looking like a cocktail waitress.

I tell Nick I'm not feeling well and have to go home. He says if I'm not well, I can't walk. He offers to drive me, which he would've done anyway. I give Lucy a hug and tell her we're right behind her. Frank and his crew will be in early to straighten up, but the volunteers' party wasn't that raucous, and everyone's neat.

When we're alone, Nick gives me a big hug. Not sexual. Warm, caring. I tell him again that I'd like to go home. We leave the building and walk across to his car. He opens my door, as always. No one else is in the garage. And I start to cry.

***

NICK

"What is it? Darling, what is it?" I reach for Lizzie.

She pulls away. "No. Just take me home."

"I will, of course. But tell me what's wrong."

"You think I'm a bimbo."

I want to laugh. Who says bimbo anymore? But I don't laugh.

Instead, "You're beautiful. So talented. And that story was good enough to be on the network."

This is exactly the wrong thing to say. Lizzie doesn't have to respond. I know what she's thinking. UBN doesn't dress Karen like a bimbo.

Lizzie has stopped crying, and in a voice so composed it's scary, says, "Please take me home."

It's only five blocks, so the silence doesn't drag on for long. Not knowing what to say, I say nothing. At the gate, Lizzie gives me her security card. We pull under the portico. I'm about to get out to open her door, but something tells me to sit still. Lizzie doesn't move. Then I figure out what to say.

"I'd like to be with you tonight. I would like more than anything in the world to take you back to my place and just hold you."

Lizzie says nothing. And then she cries again. I make no move to hold her.

Then she reaches out for my hand. "Okay."

And we drive off.

17

NICK

Lizzie Lomax is standing on my balcony. It's not particularly big. There's barely room for both of us, so I give her a minute. She's staring out at the Atlantic Ocean.

"You're right," she says. "I like Biscayne Bay better at night."

"Still, I'm glad you're here."

She turns and looks at me. Her makeup is runny from the tears. Lizzie seems to realize that and runs a hand across her cheeks.

"You've seen me in a bathing suit. And you've seen me in this dress. I'd like to show you something everyone else hasn't seen."

I pause. Now she's the one being formal, almost ceremonial, because we both sense this means so much more than simply hooking up.

"Okay," I say. "Thank you."

Lizzie half-smiles. Then she unzips her dress and lets it drop. Without waiting, she slides off her enormous panties and unhooks her bra. The room is dark except for a sliver of moon illuminating her from behind. I can't tell you how lovely she is because I'm seeing so much more, inside and out, than everyone who was watching TV.

Stepping over to me, Lizzie unbuttons my shirt and my pants. We both slip out of our shoes. The top of her head barely reaches my chest. I hold her to my heart and gently kiss her hair. She tilts back her face. We kiss forever.

I won't let Lizzie do anything for me. She wants to tell me, I know, that in a way this is selfish. Because she's so generous. But I've been selfish before with other women. All I did was take, and take, and take. Now I want to say, please, for this one night. When you've entrusted yourself to me, I want to give.

Because, Elizabeth, I love you.

18

LIZZIE

The problem with Nicholas is that he doesn't know how good he tastes. What do you expect from someone who likes burgers on toast, with no ketchup? So he treats me like an all-you-can-eat buffet, while I'm supposed to feast on, what? Kisses?

I let Nick keep doing his selfless thing until 2 a.m. Then, when he falls asleep, I go exploring. It's fascinating how a man's lower body can respond even when his upper body is snoring. But that doesn't last long. When I reach the jackpot, Nick sits up so fast you'd think he was doing calisthenics.

At 6 a.m., I'm back on Nick's little balcony, taking in the ocean. When you can actually *see* the Atlantic, it's impressive. Especially from this height. I think we're on the twentieth floor. Nick is out running. There's a miles-long boardwalk along the ocean, and he can also hop off that and jog on the beach. Nick asked me to join him. I hit him with a pillow.

His building is a couple blocks north of the Fontainebleau Hotel, where Harriet from our dance story, went for her investment seminar. Of course, the Fontainebleau is famous for other things. The Rat Pack used to hang around there. And Nat King Cole and the other black entertainers Mrs. Lewis told us about. Nick says they filmed a James Bond film by the pool. He's big into James Bond. Hence the Jaguar?

I'm hoping we can go sometime to the hotel's glitzy LIV nightclub. I don't know what LIV stands for, and gawking at A-listers is not my idea of a good time, honestly. But everyone says LIV is something to see once. And getting there's a lot easier than crawling along South Beach. Ardis has contacts at that club. Maybe we can all go together.

Meantime, I'm waiting for Nick to return so we can kiss some more before he takes me home. I'd like to get to the station by ten, when the Help Center opens. Bob Beardsley will want to talk about how last night went. I also have to review story possibilities with Lucy and Nick, but we don't have another shoot scheduled 'til Wednesday—a raid on a puppy mill. And since I'm on only the five o'clock newscast tonight, maybe Nick and I can go out for dinner. Passion and domesticity. Sigh.

***

NICK

My boss, Leland Davis, saw last night's segment. He liked it. As did my pals Harry and Joel, and my family. Also got good feedback from colleagues at my office. So a nice start.

I'll head over to the Help Center now to answer any questions I can and help choose upcoming stories.

***

LIZZIE

Well, things have gone from bad to worse. First, two volunteers, including Aunt Alicia, called in sick. We pushed everyone too hard. And we really have to train more people. Luckily, Lucy's getting calls not only from folks with problems, but also from viewers who want to help. Including Daniela Rojas. She knocked on my door after Nick brought me home this morning, said sweet things about the segment, and asked when she can start. I gave her Lucy's number.

Then Danny Fishel, our IT guy, came to the Help Center with what he thought was great news. A screen grab of me flashing on the anchor desk last night is going viral. More than three hundred thousand hits so far on YouTube alone. And you know what? I'm past caring. Almost.

And now, what is *this* about? Bob has summoned me to his office for a call from Sheryl MacDonald. She's the president of UBN News. The network's entire news division, local and national. I've never even seen her before, beyond a closed-circuit annual meeting for all the staff of the O&O's. Bob won't say what this is about. It can't be to congratulate me for getting Jorge de la Cova off the dance floor. I suspect blowback from someone powerful we're investigating. The supermarket chain? That must be it.

Bob's phone rings. He puts it on speaker.

A woman says, "Mr. Beardsley?"

He drawls, "Yes, here," then whispers to me that this is MacDonald's assistant.

"Is Ms. Lomax with you?"

"Yes, she is."

"Just a moment. I'll put Sheryl on."

We wait about thirty seconds. I look at all the resume reels stacked up in Bob's office. Reporters and anchors without agents send montages of their best stuff. Mine was one of those reels eighteen months ago. Will I have to go job-hunting again?

"Hello, Bob?" Apparently, this is Sheryl MacDonald. She sounds no-nonsense but warm, even funny.

Bob says, "Yes. Hi."

"Hi. Glad that storm's heading east. Those kind of ratings we don't need. Especially when we have such a great new franchise." MacDonald speaks a little louder. "Lizzie, are you there?"

"Yes. How do you do?"

"I do okay, but you did very well last night. Thank you."

I'm flabbergasted. And that's the first time I've ever used that word.

"Thank you for the opportunity, Ms. MacDonald."

The big boss says, "I'm sorry we're not able to see each other right now. I'm not set up for video. But maybe that's just as well, if you're wearing anything as ridiculous as what they put you in last night."

"I... you know, Ms. MacDonald, that was not my choice."

"Sheryl." She laughs. "Nobody keeps this job long enough to insist on formality. I happen to know that you raised hell about the dress. And for all the right reasons. We've invested a lot in your Help Center. Bob got the attorney general to sign on. By the way, that assistant of his is going to be a star, like you. And it cheapens the Help Center, and the station, and the whole network to make you look… well, it's not the look we're going for. Even if adolescents on social media are lapping it up. I'm glad Bob brought this to my attention."

"Bob?" I look at him and mouth, *Thank you.*

"Yes. That's why Bob's been there for eight years. Which is quite a run for news directors. And news presidents."

Bob is doing his usual man-of-few-words thing, but he's a rock.

"Here's the thing, though," Sheryl says. "Many people here think a lot of Harry Lutz. Including Steve Rosser."

He's the head of the O&O's, next in line for us after Sheryl. And Rosser is the creep who initially shot down Bob's objections. When I first kicked up about sitting on the desk in that dress, Bob warned me that I wasn't Steve Rosser's choice to head the Help Center. Sheryl MacDonald picked me. She got involved because we're guinea pigs. If a volunteer consumer center like ours plays well in Miami, the network plans to clone us for the other O&O's—from New York to LA. Sheryl noticed me because she heard I was Karen's sister. Bet that's also how I got into the gossip column.

Steve Rosser thought, maybe still thinks, that I'm too inexperienced. And maybe I am. I haven't heard from Rosser since getting the gig. Now he must have Bob Beardsley and me on his enemies list.

Sheryl continues, "There's no need to step on toes. Pick out your own clothes from now on. Do you have a clothing allowance?"

"No, I don't." They're only for anchors.

"Well, as the head of a franchise you have a clothing allowance now. Another thing. We put those giant video screens in the studio for a reason. No need for you to sit on the desk. Alicia can talk with you in front of the big screen graphics and video, don't you think, Bob?"

"I do."

Bob's not the kind of man who'd say, *Yes, I always thought so,* but I'm sure he discussed using the screens with Sheryl.

"I also wouldn't mind seeing that assistant AG on set sometimes," Sheryl says. "What's his name?"

"Nick Harris," I say.

Not Nicholas. Nick is a great TV name. Nicholas is for me.

"Is there anything else?" Sheryl asks.

"No. Thanks so much, Ms. MacDonald. Sheryl."

"I plan on coming to Miami at the end of sweeps. Look forward to seeing you, Bob. And you, Lizzie. Keep up the great work."

"Thank you," we both say.

When Sheryl hangs up, I hug Bob. It's unprofessional, but I'm a hugger and he reminds me of someone.

"My father will be grateful." I smile at Bob.

"My daughters will be, too."

<u>19</u>

LIZZIE

On Tuesday, I got a text from Karen. She missed the live broadcast of my story but promised to watch it on the website. And she apologized for not calling. Seems my sister was busting her ass to complete her own Thursday story for *Backstory*, the consumer one we talked about. I understood.

Our Wednesday package with Mrs. Lewis went well. Everybody loves her, and I found it surprising how many people around Miami don't know the sad history of Overtown. Kevin dropped in archival film clips and photos. He especially liked using Billie Holiday and other jazz greats, saying his father would get a kick out of seeing all this. And the supermarket chain did not complain. On the contrary, corporate headquarters in St. Louis issued an apology and vowed to lower Overtown prices in line with other locations. We even got the local manager to visit Ivy Lewis at her home. That featured in our new POP, a proof-of-performance promo for the Help Center. The commercial also features Nick and me. I'm now doing all my shopping at the chain's supermarket in my neighborhood. Bags and bags o' salad. Best of all, I'm no longer a pinup for acne-plagued boys on Twitter and Instagram.

Speaking of shopping. My first purchase with the clothing allowance, I went to Ardis's store, but she didn't have what I wanted at the shop or in her closet, so I got a jumpsuit from Neiman's, with a tastefully draped neckline, cap sleeves. It's too fancy for the field, but on set I look professional, elegant, and Ardis says, smashing. Four-inch heels help me pull it off. Alicia and I now meet at the big screen. We are not sex symbols. We are journalists.

The sex symbol is Nick. My boyfriend is Miami's new heartthrob. Our volunteers are besieged all day from viewers, mostly women, who want to see more of Nick on the air. And maybe off the air. Sheryl MacDonald is fine with that. So is Attorney General Davis, as well as Bob Beardsley. Bob stood by me, but you don't survive thirty-five years in the news business without racking up ratings. That's why he's tossing Nick to the wolves. And the cougars.

It's now Thursday night and Nick and I are at his place, watching *Backstory*. I wasn't sure how I'd feel about him ogling Karen. He's not, I can tell. Mostly because—as once promised—he's all over me, perhaps as reassurance. But I fight Nick off long enough to watch my sister's investigation.

This is a blockbuster. Performing its own crash test, UBN is showing how, due to faulty gas tanks, Luxor Montana pickups can explode in a fireball, even during slow-speed, low-impact collisions. Wow.

Strangely, though, Nick is cracking up. "That's the truck Leland Davis wants me to drive instead of my Jag. He has one, painted with FSU colors."

"That's terrible."

"Well, he didn't know. I hope. In fact," Nick pulls out his phone, "I'd better text him right now not to drive that pickup. Leland can be mean as a gator, but without him I wouldn't have you."

Meantime, I'm texting Kary with congratulations. She put this together brilliantly, and I hope everyone with one of those trucks saw it. This is what you can do on the network. Miami's a good-sized local market, but I don't think Bob is going to let us crash-test any vehicles.

<u>20</u>

NICK

"Invite her, of course. And don't feel you have to wait. How about taking Lizzie out in your boat? I'm surprised you haven't done that yet." This is all said in one breath.

"Mom," I say, "you have no idea how busy we are. Especially Lizzie."

"I have some idea what it is to be busy," Judge Harris says. "We do a brisk business in my courtroom."

"You have a bailiff," I note.

Ralph Haaser, who's been with Mom for five years.

"Lizzie has me."

"I see your point. The poor woman is digging up stories while you're posing for *Miami Magazine*."

Yesterday, they shot a few pictures for their Men of Style section. The bowtie is catching on. Lenny hasn't stopped teasing Lizzie about how right he was.

"You don't think inviting her is too much?" I ask my mother. "Unleashing the whole family on her? Aunt Sue."

We're discussing Thanksgiving. Bob Beardsley's been Lizzie's biggest fan, but it seems rules are rules. Even though the ratings book ends the night before the holiday, and even though Lizzie is now heading a franchise, she's still been with WTAN for only a year and a half. And that gives all the more senior reporters dibs on holidays. Many of them are from Miami and could easily fit in an early feast before going to work, so Lizzie was hoping she could swap days off. And Ileana Bonilla agreed, but then her mother fell and broke her hip, so Ileana needs to be home. Instead, Bob is rewarding Lizzie by letting her co-anchor the morning show for the first time, on Thanksgiving Day. And she thanked him for that.

Normally it wouldn't matter, because Lizzie's folks could come down to be with her. But they already booked a visit to Karen to see her newly decorated apartment. Lizzie was planning to go. Autumn in New York. Shows, restaurants. UBN is arranging VIP seats for them at Herald Square for the parade. So Lizzie and her parents, and I'm sure, Karen are disappointed. But I'm not and my mother is delighted.

As for my worries about Mom's older sister...

"Sue will be fine," she says. "As long as Lizzie doesn't object to a wedding at the club. That afternoon."

We sing, in unison, "I'm not getting any younger."

Mom and I do a mean impersonation of Aunt Sue, who isn't mean, simply desperate to spoil a grandniece or nephew. Sue's own son, Howard, is divorced with no plans to start a family.

We're sitting in the kitchen where I grew up. It's Sunday morning and Mom made breakfast. Back when I was a kid, Mom's only job was cooking. Well, supervising our cook, Marianna. Now she has another job, judging civil cases at the Miami-Dade County Courthouse.

My apartment could fit inside this kitchen. It's Mom's inner sanctum, even more than the courtyard and the pool. Her house is in Bayshore. That's across from the long strip of Miami Beach that faces the ocean. She's on the other side of Indian Creek. Geography—all of Miami Beach is separated from the City of Miami by Biscayne Bay. The house is Spanish-style, too big for Mom, and historic. My grandfather and his father before him had money, and my father still does. If he hasn't paid it all to nymphets.

My favorite room is the octagonal library. Two stories tall with red oak built-in shelves, it's the heart of the house. Or was. My father kept his collection of twenty thousand LPs and 78s there, almost all classical. I like classical music, but when he left the records went with him. I read that he's since donated them to Florida Atlantic University. For a nice tax deduction, I'm sure.

Mom and I replaced the records with books and some CDs of my own. Classical, jazz, rock, and country. That wasn't enough to fill up the room, so Mom festooned the shelves with silk flowers and carved Japanese lacquer. When it comes time to donate her collection, I bet it'll be more valuable than my father's. And more beautiful.

"What's Lizzie like?" Mom is smiling. "I mean, I've seen her on the news and she's smart and adorable. I'm so glad they let her pick out her own clothes now. What was that guy thinking? She has wonderful taste."

"She's smart. And funny. Grandma will love her—she has a huge appetite."

"You wouldn't know it."

"Wait 'til Thanksgiving. If she comes."

"I hope she will."

Mom hasn't mentioned Karen. That's why she's a judge. She's judicious. When Karen first appeared on *Backstory,* I reminded Mom that we went out in college. I'm curious to hear if she saw the truck explosion story last Thursday and what she thought about it. We're both lawyers. After my father left, Mom went to law school while I was still in grade school. I'm wondering if she's had any cases like Karen's.

Instead I ask, "So what's on that busy docket? Anything fun?"

"Fun?" Mom purses her lips and considers.

Without a gavel, she's fun in a quiet way. Since the divorce, I don't think Mom's ever quite recovered her silliness. And she's never remarried.

"Well, we do have a pirate case."

"Really?"

"Treasure hunters. I can't go into it, but tell the station to keep an eye on *Peters v. Tortuga Marine Exploration.* They can call Ralph. Is there a Help Center story in something like that?"

"I'll find out. Thanks. Meantime, I'm doing a story with Joel. You know, the guy I play tennis with. It's about his cabin cruiser."

"Didn't they ever fix that?"

"No. So we've never gone treasure hunting."

We laugh. I get up to clear the dishes.

Mom says, "You did use your own boat to recover that jewelry box. With the high school ring on the chain."

"Yeah. Did I ever tell you? I got in touch with Cooper City High, the principal's office. They put out some kind of announcement, but no one ever responded. I turned the ring in to them."

"Was it an old ring? Which class?"

"From a couple years ago. The box was bobbing in the canal. It may've been an accident, but I always imagined somebody had a bad breakup and tossed it."

"Well, I'm glad you turned it in. Hate to see you in court."

We smile and Mom drinks her coffee. She's squeezed me fresh OJ.

"Ask Lizzie about coming," she says, quietly. I can't wait to meet her."

21

LIZZIE

During our Sunday three-way call yesterday, Karen seemed fine. Her usual self. So this must be shocking her as much as it does us. It's now Monday, 8 a.m., and Mom couldn't get through to Kary, so she called me. Eight o'clock. When did they release all this?

"I don't understand," Mom says, clearly upset.

I am, too.

"Are they claiming Karen did this deliberately?" she asks. "Or could it be a mistake?"

"I don't know. Maybe when I get to the station, Bob, the news director, can tell me something."

"How would he know?" Mom asks.

"UBN may be briefing their local people. Viewers are always calling in, asking about network programs. So… I don't know."

During the pause, I put my cell phone down and put on my robe. I'm in my apartment. It was going to be a beautiful morning.

"This is terrible." Mom is on her cell, at school.

"Maybe. But don't keep trying to call Kary. She must be…"

"What?"

"Going crazy. Wait for her to call us. Does Daddy know?"

"I haven't heard from him. He's at work, too."

"Well, don't worry him."

"I have to get to class."

Mom saw all this on the TV in the teacher's lounge.

"Send me a text if you hear from Kary," I say.

"She may try to reach you first."

"Maybe. She's going to be fine, Mom. There are always two sides. Love you."

"This is not good. Love you, too."

This is BAD. All the other networks are carrying it, of course, and social media is exploding. It. Is. Everywhere.

Luxor Motors is suing UBN for defamation. They claim the *Backstory* crash test was staged, that the network rigged the truck's fuel tank to make it explode. And there's supposed to be a witness.

I'm on late tonight, so I don't have to go in 'til later. Although, we do have a shoot today—that story Nick's been wanting to do about phony debt collection.

My cell rings again and I grab it. "Nick?"

"Sweetheart?" He sounds hesitant. Of course. "Have you seen the news?"

"Yes. I just got off the phone with my mother. Are you still in the car?"

"No, I'm at the office. It's on the browser homepage."

"It's everywhere." Now I'm in front of the TV, opposite the sofa, skipping channel to channel.

The morning news shows are still on, national and local. They all have clips of the pickup truck bursting into flames. Cable news is showing Karen, but I can't hear what they're saying about her.

Nick asks, "Have you heard from—"

"No, she hasn't called. And I don't want to call her."

"Sure."

"It's not that Kary wouldn't want to talk."

"No, of course not."

"But she must be… overwhelmed."

"Look, I'm getting ready as fast as I can and going in to the station. Bob or Doug Long may know more."

"You want me to meet you?" I ask. "What time is our shoot?"

"I could push that off. We're okay for this week."

"No. It'll be good to work."

And I think how bad that sounds. Will Karen be able to work?

Nick seems to be reading my mind. He says, not confidently, "You know, Luxor may be blowing smoke. Sorry, I'm not trying to be funny."

"I know."

"They're not going to do anything to Karen until…"

"I know. Sweetheart, thanks for calling."

"Of course."

"I'll see you later."

"Lizzie?"

"Yes."

He pauses. I take a breath. I can read Nick's mind, too. He wants to say he loves me, but we haven't quite gotten that far yet. And anyway, he doesn't want to say it like this. As reassurance because I'm upset.

"I know," I say. "See you in a little while."

And we disconnect.

22

LIZZIE

Usually I walk, but Ardis drives me to the station on her way to open the store. Meg is still at sea, somewhere off South America. She'll call as soon as she hears. She's Meg. I actually wanted to walk, but Ardis insisted on taking me because she wants to tell me what villains the people all are at Luxor and UBN, and of course, the government. Ardis is a true friend, but I can't wait to climb out of her Mini.

Starting with Arlene at the reception desk, everyone smiles and greets me and then lapses into embarrassed silence. Dale, the assignment editor, discreetly turns down the volume on all five TV monitors facing his desk, all showing reports from cable networks and local competitors about *Backstory*. It's worse than gloating. Our rivals are going to milk this to show that UBN and UBN/WTAN can't be trusted. That we're out to take down innocent companies, including the one that made your car. A company that perhaps employs you. A company that represents America's industrial base. They'll suggest we're willing to screw anyone for the sake of ratings. Assuming Luxor's claim is true, and I am assuming it's true because they've scheduled a 10 a.m. news conference which everyone will be covering.

Bob's on the phone but waves me to sit down. Once again, I look at the resume reels multiplying all over his office. This time I'm not worried about my own job. But Karen's?

The supermarket chain was great about our investigation because everything Mrs. Lewis told us about their high prices was true. And we checked it out beforehand. I don't mean to sound self-righteous, but we did. In our case it was easy. All we did was compare grocery prices around town. Had the story not panned out, it would've meant nothing to drop it. I can't imagine what kind of pressure Karen was under from the network to make her much more complex story stick.

I wish she would call.

Bob's trying to wrap up his call quickly. "I've got Lizzie Lomax right here in my office. Yes. I will."

He hangs up and tries to smile at me, but Bob's smile is a work in progress in the best of times. Which these are not. He's impassive not because he's cold, but because he's seen it all, or thought he had until today.

Reading my mind—can everyone read my mind? I thought it was only Nick, and that was romantic—Bob says, "I can't believe how fast all this is moving. Never seen anything like it."

"Is Karen going to be okay?"

"You haven't spoken with her yet?"

"I didn't want to call and bother her. She hasn't even called my mother."

Bob looks at me, considering what he wants to say. "That was Steve Rosser on a conference call, briefing me and all the other news directors. Save what I'm going to tell you until the network responds officially. That won't be until after Luxor's news conference—"

"At ten."

"Right. It's bad. Rosser says there's probably going to be a corporate shake-up—"

"So what Luxor's claiming is true?"

"Seems so. We'll know more at ten."

"And Karen?"

Bob pauses. He's a straight shooter but not hasty. I'm picturing Karen doing a standup in front of the flaming rubble of the truck. Karen in her newly decorated apartment, even though I haven't seen it. And both of us as kids, my big sister telling me she got the lead in the school production of *Bye Bye Birdie*.

"Rosser didn't say," Bob replies. "But I'd be shocked if she's not suspended, at the least. Maybe let go."

I collapse in my chair, pull my lips in and begin chewing on them.

Bob says, "It all depends on how involved Karen was in that story. You and I know she may've done a couple interviews and shown up for the stand-ups. But I think they'll still have to suspend her."

I say nothing. Bob knows how I feel.

"You're supposed to go out on a story today?" he asks.

"With Nick, yes."

"How about let him do it? Or Kevin could probably shoot it himself."

"Now I feel great."

"You know what I'm saying. Unless you *want* to go out."

"I do."

Bob nods, "I would, too. What time?"

"We've got to be in Coconut Grove at noon. Debt vultures threatening an old lady with losing her house. She's nice. And frightened."

"So you see, things could be worse," Bob says, gently.

I'm told he earned two Purple Hearts and other medals in Vietnam. He worked his way up from San Antonio to UBN/Denver before the network moved him here because WTAN needed a news director with his strength. You wouldn't think a tall, tight-lipped Texan right out of a Clint Eastwood movie could get the bead on Miami. It's a unique blend of cultures and politics, the competition is fierce, and corporate pressure's intense. But Texas Ranger Bob Beardsley is as sharp as they come. And though he may do it quietly, like when he went over Rosser's head to speak with Sheryl about my clothes, Bob stands on his principles.

For instance, before the Help Center launched, I got tipped off to a teen dance club in Wynwood. They'd covered up a girl overdosing there and later dying. Fourteen years old. Turns out the place should've been called Drugs-R-Us.

The problem was, the club sponsored a Saturday afternoon show on our station. Movies with cut-ins from the DJs. I went to Bob and laid out the story but made the mistake of suggesting we might face pushback from our own sales department. Their job is tough enough without news torpedoing local moneymakers. Bob looked at me hard, the way I bet he sometimes looks at his daughters when they get wobbly, and told me to, "Go get that story." It won Kevin and me a local Emmy. And it may've saved some other kids' lives.

Nick didn't used to think so, but what we do is important, sometimes. If we do it right.

***

NICK

Well, this is devastating. The kind of case every lawyer salivates over, especially if you work on contingency. Luxor is demanding 1.9 *billion* dollars for damage to its reputation. On top of that, it's pulled all advertising from UBN and the network's owned or affiliated stations.

To substantiate those damages, at its press conference, Luxor read an affidavit from an unnamed witness—maybe someone involved with the crash test, maybe someone with UBN. The witness claims the network's outside safety expert rigged the truck's fuel tank with an incendiary device. Worse still, Luxor's own experts slowed down the *Backstory* footage and showed it at the press conference frame-by-frame. Sure enough, you could see smoke coming from the fuel tank a few seconds *before* the collision.

Worst of all, the witness led Luxor to a junkyard in New Jersey where they found the burned-out wreck. And inside its fuel tank, as photographs show, they found what was left of the incendiary device. Case closed.

I watched all this at my office. Didn't want to crowd Lizzie if she wanted to watch alone in her office, and probably talk afterward with her parents. But now I'm heading over. Bob Beardsley called and said Lizzie still wants to shoot Mrs. Leathers's interview today for our debt collection piece. She's expecting us, and she especially wanted to meet Lizzie. But Bob said if Lizzie's having a hard time, Kevin Rafael could pick up the b-roll later on his own. B-roll is all the other shots, apart from the interviews and stand-ups.

Bob is a good guy.

***

LIZZIE

My office, like Lucy's, is separated from the main room of the Help Center by glass panels. We like it that way. I get to see the volunteers, who've been terrific as always, and they get to see me. But now that Nick's here, the two of us want privacy.

The nearest place to find it is inside Frank's maintenance closet. We close the door and nearly faint. What kind of chemicals does he store in here? And does Frank ever wash out the mops? The only way to stay conscious is by pressing our noses together and kissing. I hope my sister has someone like this in New York.

<u>23</u>

LIZZIE

"This isn't a shakeup," Nick whispers to me. "It's an earthquake."

We're in the studio with the rest of WTAN's staff, from the anchors to Frank's maintenance crew, who brought out dozens of folding chairs. Jack Borch, the chairman of our parent company is holding a press conference. It's on all the networks and my parents are probably watching, if they can get free at work. Everyone here at the station is watching it closed-circuit on one of the studio's giant screens. Our general manager, Doug Long, wants us all together to hear this.

Borch announced that three *Backstory* producers have been dismissed, including Lisa Nape. Also, that Sheryl MacDonald has "resigned" as president of UBN News. And that the parent company and UBN are already in settlement talks with Luxor Motors, only five hours after Luxor's press conference. Jack Borch concludes by saying, "The best thing to do when we make a mistake is to admit it."

But no mention of Karen.

We all silently file back to our work places. Four Help Center volunteers had to keep answering calls, so we fill them in.

Half the calls all day have been about *Backstory*. Some people say they'll never watch UBN again. We can only apologize and say we hope they'll change their mind. Other callers want updates. There's always someone calling a TV station, even with the Internet, for updates on something, or personal weather reports, or simply to chat. And that's fine, especially when they sound lonely.

Then there was one lady in Margate who called while we were out shooting to say she hoped Karen Lomax and her sister were okay. Lucy gave me Dorothy Eiger's number and I called back to thank her.

I am not okay. I haven't heard from Karen and neither has Mom. We still aren't calling or texting her, but Dad says he's ready to jump on a plane for New York. Short of that, if there's still no word, Dad's going to call her tonight. Karen always answers Dad.

You may think it's selfish to be thinking this, but Sheryl MacDonald's resignation—if it was a resignation and not a firing—is also a personal blow. That phone call in Bob's office was the first and only time we spoke, but Bob let me know that all this time, she's been a secret mentor. Now Sheryl's gone and we don't know who's going to replace her. All we can do is hunker down and try to have a great ratings book. Bob and Doug have been kind enough to say that it's pretty great so far, thanks in some measure to the Help Center. We may get even bigger numbers in the wake of this *Backstory* scandal. Soap operas beat out news.

By the way, this is the first day in the Help Center for Daniela Rojas. My neighbor managed, amid the uproar, to sneak in a little training from Lucy. And as a new member of our team, Daniela went to the studio with the rest of us to watch the press conference. Daniela looked at me pityingly, but the nice thing about having the wife of *El Cocodrilo* on your team is that she's seen way worse.

***

<u>NICK</u>

"What the hell is going on down there?" My boss is calling from the state capital.

I'm back in my own office, giving Lizzie space. "Leland, I can't tell you anything more than you've seen on the news."

"You can't, or you won't tell me? You're still working for me, boy."

"Hey," I protest. "That's out of line. Did you get my text during *Backstory,* about your truck?"

"Thank you for saving my life. Although now it seems my life was never in a bit of danger. However, the reputation of this office most certainly is, 'cause you're working with a bunch of crooks."

"Nobody down here is a crook or a con-artist or anything else. For Christ's sake, Leland, you've seen the stories we're putting on the air."

"I've seen you modeling bowties."

"You're the one who talked me into doing this."

"Well, now I see it may be a bad idea."

We both hold fire for a minute. If Mr. Attorney General wants to pull me, that's fine. I'm that mad. Except, it would make things even tougher for Lizzie.

I crumple up a sheet of paper and throw it toward the trash basket and miss. Hope that wasn't anything important.

"So what's next?" Leland asks. "That MacDonald woman who helped set this whole thing up. She's out now?"

"I can't believe she knew anything about that crash test."

"Oh, you can't believe. Only you're not on the jury. There will be no jury. MacDonald was kicked out on her ass, and they're buying their way out of this mess—for God knows how many millions—faster than a speeding ticket up here in Tallahassee. Where people are not slow. So don't tell me the network didn't know they're guilty as sin." Davis takes a breath. "Who's replacing MacDonald?"

"Haven't heard."

"I've got a call in to Jack Borch's office. Met him at a fundraiser a couple years ago. Of course, who knows how long he's got a job. Or how long I'll be around. But if I get any shit over this, Harris, you're going to answer for it. So don't frame anyone else to boost that damn station's ratings. Or to impress your girlfriend."

"What—"

"Yes, I know all about that. Why do you think we have an investigative division? All right, quiet down."

The damn fool seems to be talking to himself. Good, because I've stopped listening.

"Look," Davis says, finally, "we're gonna ride this out 'til the dust settles. And then I'll see."

"Can I remind you one last time that WTAN and the Help Center have absolutely nothing to do with blowing up trucks?"

"Tell that to your viewers. Who are also voters." And the attorney general hangs up.

<u>24</u>

LIZZIE

"You sound as though you don't believe me," Karen says.

"I don't," I reply. Adding quickly, "I mean, I don't sound that way. I *do* believe you, of course."

Our voices are both up an octave and louder than usual. That's shocking from Karen, because she's been confident and composed since junior high, when everyone except her had pimples. We're both trying to convince each other. But do I believe her?

Kary finally called back Mom and Dad around 11:15 tonight. I was on the air, so Mom sent me a text saying Karen would stay up, waiting for me to call her after my show. That's all the text said, so I don't know what they discussed.

After the Help Center segment, I called Karen immediately from my office, and after what seemed like forever, she picked up. And sounded reluctant to talk.

Kary has never felt like she was competing with me. That she ever had to measure up, much less answer to me. She's three years older. She's all the things you see on TV, and lots more. If she's ever felt any pressure *vis-à-vis* me, it's the pressure to live up to a kid sister's hero worship. That's why it's been hard to believe Nick could be interested in me. He had Karen.

Yet now, Kary's on the defensive and being kind of mean about it. What Bob Beardsley would call, *as jumpy as a rattler gettin' poked with a stick*. But I'm not poking. Maybe it's wrong right now to ask, but I'm trying to understand how it's possible to turn your story so completely over to a producer that something like this could happen. And how could you not know about it? I don't ask about any of that. But my sister guesses.

"Lizzie, forgive me," Karen says, in a weary voice, "but you don't know what it's like to work for a network. I'm not saying you'll never make it. But for now, you're local."

Glancing through the glass panels of my office, into the empty Help Center, I see it through Karen's eyes. She wouldn't be impressed.

"I used to be local, too," she continues. "In Houston, a bigger market than Miami. So we both know local reporters do everything themselves, because they have to. Even O and O's usually doesn't hire field producers like Lisa Nape. But when you work for a news magazine, the pressure is completely different. I do as much as I can, but," Karen's voice is on the rise again, "this was a technical engineering story. How was I supposed to supervise what anyone was doing to a fuel tank? That's why we have experts and producers."

I start to say something, but Karen adds, "Not only that, *Backstory* had me working on four stories at once. Besides fluff like the Duchess interview, which had me appearing on every UBN news show and dozens of local ones."

"Okay," I soothe. "You don't have to—"

"Thank you, Lizzie," Karen mocks. "Thank you for understanding. But you still don't understand."

I hear Karen taking a sip of something. She coughs, then goes on explaining.

"*Backstory* does magazine stories. Long form stories that we shoot all over the country. All over the world. I'm not crossing my legs in a micro-mini skirt on a desk in Miami and tossing to a ninety-second package. Yeah, I finally saw the dance lesson thing."

I hope what Karen's drinking is alcoholic and she's buzzed, because this is so unkind that for a moment I'm stunned.

"I don't have to sit on the desk anymore."

"Well, I'm glad of that. Because it was embarrassing. For me. I'm trying to be serious—"

"And I'm at least trying to tell the truth."

Now Karen is stunned. When she speaks again, she's using not only her indoor voice, but the professional voice. I'm getting frozen out. And if you're like Nick—my joking version of Nick—and thinking of the sisters in the Disney movie *Frozen*, well I am, too.

Maybe Karen's always been this way and I never noticed. She never had to reveal it. What do they say? Crisis reveals character.

That professional voice is something Karen has been working on slowly but with great patience for many years, long before she got into broadcasting. Our dad's family's originally from Kentucky, so there's some country left in his speech. Mom loves English literature, but she never used that as an excuse to sound like the landed gentry, even when she was reading aloud Jane Austen or the Brontës. Although, when Mom read Harry Potter to us, she tried doing what we called *the voices*. Her Hagrid was classic.

Karen's budding professional voice—she'd used by the time she'd reached senior year in high school and had polished it so it gleamed—wasn't ridiculous. Nothing about Karen ever approached the ridiculous. Yet even more than her looks and her accomplishments, that voice made Karen different from the other kids. If she'd never gone on television, Karen could've made it in radio. Or doing voice-overs for deluxe products.

Everyone in our school was more or less the same when it came to money and houses and clothes. Some kids' parents, though, were professionals. And that rankled Karen. She hated having Mom hanging around all the time in high school, although Karen was never in Mom's class. And before, in middle school, Mom says Karen embarrassed Dad. It was career day and the police department sent Dad, knowing he had a daughter there. A lot of the kids, and not only boys, gathered around the police display, handling unloaded guns and tasers and asking Dad how many people he'd shot. The answer was none, which they didn't believe. But Karen avoided Dad's table like it was radioactive. She didn't even say hello.

Apparently, this got worse in college. Karen did meet a lot of rich kids at Vanderbilt, including Nick. She joined the most exclusive sorority, Kappa Alpha Theta. She went out with Nick for two months, and I gather it was hot and heavy. But Nick says Karen never talked about her family. Whenever he asked, she changed the subject. He didn't know our father was a cop until Dad got shot. Karen came right home and she couldn't have been more upset or more caring, but then Karen and Nick broke up. She called it off, Nick insists. He hastened to add, before I kicked him, that breaking up was the best thing that ever happened because he later met me.

What Karen did talk about, Nick recalls, was someday living in a New York brownstone, shopping at Bergdorf, pinky-fingering high tea at the Plaza, and jogging through Central Park. The only part of Karen's dream that appealed to Nick was running. He'd been to New York many times and found it ugly. If he couldn't live in South Florida, which he always loved, his second choice was Paris. He speaks French, like Karen.

I've never been to Paris, and I don't speak French. I've also never been ashamed of being the daughter of a cop. Except maybe once. Another Cincinnati officer shot and killed a suspect in Over-the-Rhine, a predominantly black neighborhood. Eyewitness accounts and later evidence showed that the suspect was unarmed and even had his hands up. The streets erupted. Protesters said this was only the latest in a string of unprovoked police shootings.

But some of the other shootings they cited were not fair. One involved a female officer sitting in her cruiser, when a man flung open the door, grabbed her gun, shot her in the leg, shoved her into the passenger seat while he zoomed off. The officer managed to wrestle her gun back and kill the suspect. Katie Hardaway recovered but was branded by the media as a cop who hunted down young black men.

When the riots subsided, the feds came in to restructure and monitor Cincinnati's police department. I wish I could say I stood by Dad, but a lot of my high school friends, white and black alike, came down on the police. I tried to keep my head down. I even tuned out Mom when she talked to me in a way she never had before, about how much she feared that every time Dad went out on patrol, he'd never come home again.

As an adult, one who's worked with a load of cops, I'm proud of my father. And I hope Karen is, too.

Now, on the phone we're both quiet. I'm glad I made this call from my office landline and not one of the video apps, because I don't think either of us wants to see the other's face. It would be too uncomfortable.

"Have you talked about this with Nick?" Karen asks.

With all that's going on, she's thinking about Nick?

"Yes," I say. "He was here for the press conference. He's kind of on our staff. Why? Does it matter?"

"Of course it matters." And now she's not arrogant, although the words might sound that way. "When you get... famous," Kary says, quietly, "everyone knows about you. Especially if you screw up. Or seem to have screwed up. And God knows what's going to happen to you. But none of that matters as much as wondering what people who really know you, or did really know you—who once were important to you—what's important is what they think."

"Nick thinks you're fabulous, Kary. The first time I ever saw him, he was staring at you on one of the TV sets in the lobby at my station and I thought he was going to... I don't know. He looked at you the way he must've looked at you back at Vanderbilt. I'm still trying to get over how he looked at you. The way everyone does, and not just because you're gorgeous—"

"Lizzie—"

"No, it's true. Not just because you're gorgeous, but because you work so hard and you've accomplished so much. You're not only famous, Kary. You're Karen Lomax. Kids in journalism schools all over the country want to be like you. I do, too. I'm proud of you, Kary. I always have been, and I always will be."

I think she's crying. Then she stops.

Finally, I ask, "So what's next? At least they didn't say anything about you at that press conference."

"They're not going to." And now Karen sounds different. Like she did a few minutes ago. "The network has a lot invested in me and they know I did *nothing wrong*. Steve Rosser told me I'm not being suspended." Then she wavers a little. "I'm going to be reassigned."

"Rosser?" I ask, puzzled.

Steve Rosser is head of the local stations owned by UBN.

"What does he have to do with this? You're with the network, not the O and O's."

Silence.

Karen does something I have trouble doing. What people like Bob Beardsley do so well. She gathers her thoughts instead of blurting something out. Which makes all the mean things she said to me before that much more painful.

"Look," she says. "don't talk with anyone about this. Not Mom and Dad. Not Nick Harris—"

"Nick and I—"

"Not Nick," she says emphatically. "No one. I may be working more closely with Steve Rosser. That's all I can say. And now I have to go."

"Kary."

"What," she snaps.

"I'm sorry. I really am."

"For what?"

I pause, in disbelief. "For what you're going through."

"I'm fine. Remember, Lizzie, it's a cutthroat business. Good night."

And she hangs up.

<u>25</u>

NICK

Finally. My cell rings and there's her name.

"Sweetheart?"

"No. It's Ardis."

"Is Lizzie okay? Why are you—"

"I'm using Lizzie's phone not because I forgot to charge my own, but because Lizzie has been soaking in our tub for what seems like the past eight hours. I called in and she answered. I'm afraid to peek in, because by now she must be as wrinkly as Deadpool."

"But she sounds all right?"

"No, Sherlock. Lizzie's taken up residence in the tub. She sounds depressed. That's why I'm calling you."

It's Saturday afternoon. Lizzie didn't answer my calls, so I was about to drive to her place, when Ardis rang. This is the first time she and I have actually spoken. When Ardis threatened to cut off my balls, she had left a voicemail and I'd heard her posh-plus accent, but today she's making the Queen sound like a cockney.

"You're not at your store?" I ask.

"Obviously not. We don't keep our tub at my shop. I ran home for fabric samples and found Lizzie still submerged."

"I'm coming over."

"Ardis?" That's Lizzie's voice, I'm guessing, coming from the bathroom.

Ardis warbles, "Yes, luv."

"Who are you talking to?"

"It's a crank call."

"What?"

"Be right there, Liz. Ringing off now." Ardis yells, "No, I will not give you my Social Security number. And I do not believe you speak for disabled veterans. Buzz off." Ardis calls again to Lizzie, "Are you all right, darling?"

"Yes."

"Then give me a moment. I'm stepping onto the balcony for a breath of air." Pause. Ardis whispers, "Nick?"

I hear the glass door sliding shut.

"Yes?"

"Listen, and no interruptions or stupid questions like, *Is Lizzie all right?* If you truly care for her, you would know she's not all right. So before this phone runs out of battery—because Lizzie's no better than I am—be quiet and listen. I'm going to LIV tonight. Do you know what that is?"

"Yes, the club at the Fontainebleau. I live—"

"Listen! I've been wanting to take Lizzie for ages, but she's afraid it's a pick-up joint. Which, of course, it is. Every place is, if you're lucky. I want to take Lizzie with me tonight, with you as our escort."

"All right."

"All right?" Ardis seems surprised. "Lizzie said you would hate it."

"Why?" I know why.

"Because you're a toff."

"What's a toff?" I think I know.

"An aristocratic prick. Or someone who acts like one."

I'm hurt. "Lizzie still says that about me?"

"Still?"

"Well," I admit, "I did act like a prick in the beginning."

"Do you still wear bowties?"

"When the occasion demands."

"The occasion never demands, unless you're waiting tables."

"Look, Ardis, if that's where Lizzie wants to go—"

"That's where everyone wants to go."

"Then we're going," I say, as emphatically as you can say anything to this woman before she zings you. "Two questions. Since Lizzie said yesterday that she wanted the night off, I was getting together tonight with a pal. Harry."

"Like the prince?" she asks.

"Separated at birth. Harry Mattis actually used to work at LIV. So—"

"Bring him. If he's another toff—"

"He's not."

"If he *is*, I'm good at making new friends."

"So I've heard." Shouldn't have said that.

"Really?" Ardis says, icily. Then I hear her slide the door open and yell, "Lizzie, go ahead and stay in the tub." She closes the door and says to me, "I'll deal with her in a moment. And here I am trying to cheer the girl up."

I ask, "What time can I pick you up?"

"No need. LIV doesn't really take off 'til at least half-past eleven. I have my own car. A Mini."

"Okay," I say. "I live a couple blocks up from the club, so I'll be looking for you at valet. Harry will be waiting, too."

"What does Harry look like?"

"You can't miss him."

"But—"

"See you at eleven-thirty."

"But—"

***

LIZZIE

Tracy Dinkler was chronically depressed. As our school's biggest *Twilight* fan, she wore nothing but black through all of ninth grade, when Bella chose Edward instead of Jacob. Luckily, before the start of tenth grade, Jacob imprinted on Bella and Edward's daughter, so Tracy returned to pastels. If all this means nothing to you, you weren't a girl hung up on vampires. Like I was.

Unlike Tracy, even during the toughest times, everyone says I'm chronically cheerful. In my family, I am the peacemaker. Remember, in newsrooms I bring the donuts. So what's knocked me flat now?

Karen says she'll be fine. I believe her. Sheryl MacDonald no longer has my back, but Bob Beardsley does. And Thanksgiving will be fine, too. I meet new people all the time. It's part of the job and I've never been shy. A little uncertain at times, but not a coward. Nick tells me his family will think I'm wonderful—his wealthy, high-powered, intimidating family. And if they don't, there's always Thanksgiving football.

The combination of everything this week depressed me for a while. But I'm now stepping out of the tub, and—

"Why did you tell Nick I sleep around?"

"What? Ardis, hand me a towel!"

She hands me a washcloth. "I want you to be naked when you confess." She's only half-joking.

I lunge past her, knocking down three trays of cosmetics—don't worry, we have plenty more—and grabbing a towel on my own.

Ardis is still talking. "What will this wanker Harry think of me?" She takes a breath. "What does Harry look like?"

Oh, my God. What do I look like? Bloody hell, as Ardis is too nice to say. The bathroom mirror reveals a five-foot-two-inch raisin. Deep breath.

"I've never met Harry," I say, calmly, wrapping the towel around me so tight that Ardis can't whip it off. "But Nick says he's great."

"Why will no one tell me what this man looks like?"

"Ardis, don't be superficial. What does it matter what he looks like?"

"Because he could look like you." She wrinkles her nose to show how every inch of me is wrinkled.

"You know, Ardis, I was thinking how kind it was of you not to comment on my appearance. But sure enough…" I let that hang balefully and reach for my hairbrush, which is behind Ardis. Preparing to wrestle for it, I grit my teeth. "Why the hell are we talking about Harry?"

"Because," Ardis politely hands me the brush, "we four are going clubbing tonight."

"With Nick? And Harry? Where?"

"Oh," Ardis touches-up her pink coral lip-gloss, "some dive where Harry once worked. I think it's called… LIV."

"What? When did you talk with Nick?"

"When I thought you were trying to drown yourself. Poppet, we have a whole ocean. Why do you have to tie up the bathroom?"

***

NICK

"What does she look like?" Harry wants to know.

"Ardis must be about half the size of you. Who isn't? Look, if you want to check her out, she's heading back to her store, Bermuda Blues."

"On Ocean Drive?"

"Somewhere in South Beach."

Harry and I are out on my boat, a twenty-five-foot Starcraft Crossover. The hull's blueberry, with a red stripe. They call it a crossover because you can ski or fish, or zip around, which is what we're doing. I don't fish, and if Harry tried to water ski he'd cause a tidal wave. We're enjoying the clear sky, calm sea and mild breeze on Biscayne Bay. And as it happens…

"That's where they live." I point.

"Which one?" Harry shields his eyes.

"The three white buildings. Theirs is on the right."

"You have binoculars?"

"Come on." I throw a life vest at him. "You haven't even met Ardis yet and you're already… what's the verb for voyeur?"

"Peep. To peep."

"Harry, this is Ardis. Ardis, meet Peeping Harry. Oh, this is going to go well."

***

LIZZIE

The question now is, what am I going to wear? I can't charge clubwear to my clothing allowance. And my personal clothing budget was blown on the frilly bikini and filmy yellow dress.

The answer—I'll steal something from my roommate's closet. Wait. The same roommate who arranged this whole evening? How could I do that? Because Ardis has returned to work, and I'm broke and incorrigible. And envious. A black velvet mini and strappy stilettoes I already have. But Ardis owns a silver rhinestone top, backless with a plunging neckline, and I've longed for it since she unpacked. Therefore, if Ardis isn't planning to wear it—or even if she is, since she's a fixture at LIV and this is my first time—that's mine. And Kim and Kanye, J Lo and everyone else on the dance floor better wear sunglasses, because I will be dazzling.

***

NICK

We've stepped into a lavish, garish, futuristic video game. Wow. LIV's hype is justified. Stratospheric ceilings. A dome that looks like a giant spider. And it's changing constantly because of the lights, hyper-intense red and blue lasers. A throbbing beat assaults you from everywhere. It's ear-shattering. The stars tonight are Stevie J and Don P, both DJs. I like live musicians, but Harry says canned is the way this place rolls unless there's a private party and they hire singers and a band.

Thanks to Harry, we waltz right in. He worked security here and knows the guys at the door. But the ladies we're with are so beautiful that, even without Harry, LIV would've been happy to have us.

Lizzie is sending out sparks in her mirrored top. Ardis is a knockout, too. She has short black hair and striking, turned-up blue eyes, and her dress is sort of Japanese. When Ardis stretched a leg out of her pink Mini, Harry got so flustered he tried to hide. Fat chance. When Ardis saw Harry looming overhead, she nearly fell back into the car. Harry sucked it up, reached for her the way a bear reaches for honey, and even Lizzie and I could see something clicked when these two made contact. Lizzie's smile is now brighter than her dress.

***

LIZZIE

I AM HAVING THE BEST TIME. Everyone is sparkling, especially Ardis. She's rocking a gray geisha sheath with a slit that has Harry gaping. I plan on stealing that next.

This is the first time Ardis and I have met Harry. He's an ex-Marine. You're not supposed to say *ex,* because once a Marine, always a Marine, even if you now own your own security firm, which as everyone knows, Harry does. Everyone knows that because Harry is wearing a black T-shirt advertising Semper Fi Security. For him, there is no dress code, especially since he knows the bouncers. I think Nick said he used to be a bouncer. Judging from the muscles bulging beneath that tee, Harry never had to bounce anyone. They just fled.

Ardis is also meeting Nick for the first time. When he leans in to kiss her cheek, she grabs his crotch with one hand and makes a scissor motion with the other. When I ask what the hell that was all about, she says, "Inside joke." She also explains that Nick is conventionally handsome, while Harry is elemental.

Ardis is ordering drinks. She knows the bartender. Nick thought I didn't see, but he slipped Ardis a credit card. Now he's trying to reserve a table. First, though, even Nick has to take out a bank loan.

I don't mean to be crass, but do you know what things cost here? How do all these people afford it? They're not celebs. I don't see any, although there's a rumor that Justin Bieber and Hailey Baldwin are cuddling in the back. For the rest of us, fifty bucks to get in, fifteen for a drink, and the cheapest table? Nick didn't want to tell me, but I've already learned how to wheedle things out of Harry. I promised him Ardis's number. He tells me tables start at fifteen-*hundred* dollars. I tell Nick that's too much. He says it's a special occasion. I ask, what? He says, for the first time since the Luxor press conference, I look happy again. I say, the attorney general's office must pay better than TV.

By the way, being on local TV doesn't make us A-listers, especially here. Most young people don't watch local news unless a storm's brewing.

We get the table, but Ardis immediately wants to get up and dance. It is a dance club. Still, I think we ought to sit at this exorbitantly priced table for a while and then take it home. There's another problem. The dance floor is more crowded than a Tokyo subway.

But I hadn't figured on Harry. He leads the way and the crowd parts like the Red Sea. In fact, while most dancers barely have enough room to jump up and down, those surrounding Harry and our group give him a wide berth. This gives us a chance to cut loose. Even Nick. Where does this come from? He doesn't drink alcohol. He's not smoking anything. There must be a full moon.

DJ Stevie is mixing new stuff with vintage electro funk while Ardis and Harry dance like it's Chuck Berry. They do the twist from *Pulp Fiction*. Ardis and her black bob looking sinister with alternating hand masks. When it's my turn with Nick, we of course, cha-cha-cha, Nick doing a wicked impression of Jorge de la Cova. I don't try to look like one of Jorge's eighty-year-old girlfriends. I try to look like *Dancing with the Stars*, and Nick seems to think it's working. We segue into a tango, and then Ardis and Harry join us for a line dance that's part-Texas, part-Rockettes, and then everyone on the floor joins in. I can't believe we're leading a rave.

When the four of us finally run out of call and response moves, Stevie J and Don P call for a round of applause. The boys gallantly hold our hands and bow while Ardis and I curtsy.

26

NICK

We pair off at valet. Lizzie and I are walking along the beach, back to my place. Ardis and Harry have to decide which of their vehicles to drive. Ardis shows she has some feelings for Harry by not making him squeeze into the Mini. The valets know Harry and promise to look after Ardis's car. They do this not out of fear, but friendliness. Harry is well-liked and respected. Of course, they didn't see him dance.

Lizzie hugs Ardis. I reach up and pat Harry's back, and then they roar off in his old Hummer, painted camouflage.

***

LIZZIE

The waves are lapping and the moon is full. Moon over Miami. I hiccup and apologize.

Nick's a good sport. Whatever kind of music he truly does like—what did Karen say, big bands, bagpipes—I could tell LIV and its DJs aren't Nick's thing. Yet he seemed to enjoy going crazy, the way I guess Nicholas would more often if he drank anything but iced tea. And he liked introducing Harry to a woman who's nicer than she lets on. Thank you, Ardis. So why does Nick close-up again?

We could've walked north from the Fontainebleau, along the boardwalk, but we're taking off our shoes and wading up to our knees in the surf. This is brave of me.

"You know," I say to Nick, with a false laugh, "I've been afraid of the ocean at night ever since watching the original *Jaws* on

Netflix. And now, *The Meg*." Meg is a prehistoric shark that makes the rubber fish in *Jaws* look like a guppy.

Nicholas mulls this over in his maddeningly analytical way. "If you're afraid of sharks, why watch those movies?"

I roll my eyes. "Why does anyone watch horror flicks?"

"So they can have nightmares?"

"So they can *deal* with their nightmares."

He considers. "So thanks to those movies, you're now afraid a shark will swim onto the beach."

"It's been known to happen."

It did in the Bahamas.

Nick considerately moves away from the water. He is considerate. So why am I snapping at him? Yes, I'm a little tired. Too much time in the tub. And a little buzzed. And unreasonably peeved.

"Anyway," I grumble, "I tell you about my fear of sharks, but you never tell me anything."

"About what?"

"Well, like why Karen says you were formal back in college. And you're still formal."

"I didn't feel so formal tonight on the dance floor."

"No. But what about your father? What kind of problem do you have with your father?"

Nick takes a breath. "He's gone."

"Out of the picture."

"A long time ago. There's nothing to tell."

Okay. But this is the main thing Nick won't tell me. "Why did you and my sister break up?" And I ask silently, *Do you want to get back together? Because I think she does.*

"Elizabeth," Nick says, tenderly. It's the first time he's called me that. "When I'm with you, I can't even remember who she is."

We kiss.

"Who?" I ask.

"What's-her-name."

It gets passionate. Our toes are being tickled by sea foam. A salty breeze ruffles my hair. After coming up for air, I see clouds drifting past stars. Then our lips make love again.

Nick's apartment now feels like home. It's the only place where I can sleep in a bed. Even when she's away, I don't invade Meg's bedroom. My roommate Meg, not the shark.

But we don't sleep, since there's no need to dream.

<u>27</u>

LIZZIE

It's Sunday and the family's three-way Skype call is surreal. For one thing, Dad is the first to appear. No skulking in his Barcalounger to avoid comment on his weight. Fact is, Dad's dropped about ten pounds. Yet instead of looking healthy, he seems wan but determined to be jolly.

No talk at all of Karen's work or anything else that's been all the buzz everywhere. Instead, Dad, Mom, and Karen plan for Thanksgiving in New York. Kary got them tickets to *Hamilton*, which Dad may or may not enjoy. Sometimes he surprises us. Also *The Fantasticks*, the first show Mom and Dad saw together. Their wedding song was a sweet one from the show called, "They Were You." Mom used to sing it to Kary and me as a lullaby, and I remember the ending, about how her wildest dreams were multiplied by two.

In the theater, Mom will get misty-eyed. Dad may be blubbering.

Kary and Mom also want to skate at Rockefeller Center. And of course, shop. Dad wants to see the World Trade Center memorial and the Statue of Liberty from a Circle Line boat. They all do.

In unison, my family says how much they wish I could be with them. My feelings are mixed, after that last phone call with Karen. We love each other and always will. And I want to be there for my sister. Now, though, she needs space. I do, too.

No one asks about my Thanksgiving. I don't know if Mom told Karen that I'm spending it with Nick and his family. Mom and I talked last week, with Dad making his usual noises off. Here's how that conversation went.

Mom asked, "Is this the first time you're meeting his mother? Did you say she's a judge?"

"Yes, a county court judge."

"Doubt judges down there respect the Constitution. They're all transplants from New York."

Guess who contributed that.

"Meaning they don't respect gun rights?" I teased.

That brought Dad into view.

"Hi, Daddy."

"Listen," his big face was six inches from the camera, "I don't expect you to debate politics at Thanksgiving. Nobody should. *That* leads to shootings. But if the Second Amendment didn't guarantee citizens the right to protect themselves, I'd be the only thing standing between them and armed criminals."

"Does Nick ever talk about his father?" Mom asked, oblivious to Dad's tirade.

I told her before that the Harrises are divorced.

"No. I don't think he's seen his father in many years."

"That's terrible," Dad said.

"Well, it's not something Nick chose. He was a kid when it happened."

Dad shook his head and retreated to his chair.

That was three days ago. But today, on this call with Karen, we're all as cheerful as I always try to be. Mom and Dad probably figure Karen doesn't want to hear about an old boyfriend, especially one Mom raved about when she saw Nick on TV. I understand and want Karen to be happy.

<u>28</u>

LIZZIE

Whoosh. That's how this week's felt, the last of the November ratings book. As I told you, we always try staying ahead of schedule, but the Help Center has proved such as hit that Bob Beardsley asked if we could crank out an extra story for Tuesday night. That meant airing Nick's debt collection package with Mrs. Leathers on Monday. She's not losing her home, and although we don't usually put this kind of thing in our stories, she offered a testimonial to the Help Center, including a kiss for Nick.

For Tuesday we chose a call from newlyweds about their used car. It's had constant problems since they bought it a month ago. I won't say which model, because it wasn't the manufacturer's fault. When Jim and Becky's mechanic did a deep dive, he found it was a flood car, meaning one that had been stuck in a flood. Nick and I searched records and found, sure enough, that the car was in Houston when Hurricane Harvey drenched the city with four feet of rain. The seller never told Jim and Becky.

We interviewed them. Becky's an ER nurse and Jim's in public relations. This was the first car they bought together. Kenny, the mechanic, was honest and willing to go the extra mile. We included Kenny's son, eight-year-old Ken III. Also Pops, Ken Senior, who opened the garage thirty years ago. All three Kens said, off camera, that they could get me a deal on a steal that isn't a flood car, and when I save enough I may take them up on that. Can't bum rides off Nick and Ardis forever.

Nick slid under the jacked-up vehicle with Kenny, who offered advice about how to inspect used cars before you buy.

Of course, "No one does inspections as good as my dad." That testimonial came from Ken III.

Jim and Becky got a full refund from the dealer, who wouldn't go on camera.

Tonight—the night before Thanksgiving and the end of the ratings book—we have Joel and his lemon of a cabin cruiser. You wouldn't think a story about a boy toy out of the reach of most viewers would appeal to a wide audience, but Bob Beardsley said we shouldn't discriminate against the rich, especially when you can show the rich getting screwed. Anyway, Joel and Shirley are not rich. The *Eye Eye* was their reward for tens of thousands of eyeglasses. Joel, you may remember, is an optometrist and Shirley runs the office. They weren't able to have children, so the boat and a little Yorkie named Brutus are their babies.

Nick, by the way, will tell viewers that Joel's a friend, but that Shirley filed their complaint with the AG's office long before we opened the Help Center. Nick then explains how viewers can file their own complaints.

***

NICK

Joel's case is still being investigated by my office and also by ODI, the federal Office of Defects Investigation. So no resolution to report yet. But following Joel's story, Lizzie's going to air a brief follow-up tonight on Jorge de la Cova. Looks like he's fox trotting off to jail. Even though Harriet helped nail Jorge, she's heartbroken.

"What can I say?" she tells us on camera. "For the first time since my Herbie died, Jorge made me want to dance."

The lesson here—had he been happy with a fair price for lessons and the occasional free meal, Jorge could still be dancing. Don't be greedy. And, clients, don't be too needy.

***

LIZZIE

I've been shopping. No, not for myself. Bob gave us a nice budget to throw a party for the volunteers tonight. He, John McIntyre, and Alicia will be joining us after the early news shows.

But as Nick and I carry all the bags and boxes into the Help Center, Aunt Alicia cries out to me, *"Traidor. Enemiga occulta."*

"What!" I ask Lucy, "What is she saying?"

"It's not good," Lucy says.

"Perra."

I know what that means. Bitch. I walk up to Aunt Alicia. She meets me halfway.

I beg her, "What's going on?"

She throws a copy of the newspaper on the volunteer table. The Help Center has opened, but the only volunteer still answering all the ringing phones is my neighbor, Daniela. And even she's looking at me with regret.

The paper is open to the gossip column. I pick it up, warily. Nick reads next to me. This is the lead item…

*Talk about a safe landing, and right here in our town, **Karen Lomax**'s career appeared to have gone up in flames, along with the Luxor truck that exploded after a rigged crash-test on **Backstory**. But despite her suspension from the news magazine, UBN insists Karen knew nothing about the scheme that cost the network untold millions to settle. And now I have learned that Karen Lomax is heading here. To UBN's Owned and Operated WTAN to become **John McIntyre**'s new co-anchor.*

*What does this mean for **Alicia Balart**? Karen may not have blown up that truck, but it looks like lovely Alicia's job will be part of the wreckage. And yes, as we've told you, Karen is the big sister of **Lizzie Lomax**. She's been solving consumer disputes on WTAN's Help Center segments along with that bow-tied hottie from the Attorney General's office, **Nick Harris**.*

Let's see if viewers want a sister act or Alicia's return.

My gaze snaps from the paper to Aunt Alicia, who's still cursing in English and Spanish. After looking around and finding that none of the volunteers are willing to look me in the eye, it's obvious they think I hid this from them.

"When I think," Aunt Alicia roars, "how I've worked, how we've *all* worked—yes, to help the people and our communities— but how you and *tu novio* grabbed *toda la gloria*—"

"You and your boyfriend grabbed all the glory," Lucy whispers, in translation.

"That's not fair," I protest.

"And you don't have *la decencia…*"

"The decency."

"…to tell us—to tell *me*, her aunt—the one who got this whole Center off the ground with the story of that rat of a dance instructor—you don't have the decency to tell me that your sister is stealing my beautiful niece's job."

"*Stop, please, Tia Alicia.*" Alicia, our anchor, had come into the Help Center. "I don't think Lizzie knew. Did you know?" she asks me.

"No, I didn't. Not until your aunt showed me the paper."

Alicia turns to Lucy and the volunteers. It's early and she's wearing no makeup, which makes her look prettier than ever, though clearly distraught. I realize for the first time that she's not so much older than I am.

"Listen to me, please, everyone," Alicia says. "I found out about this yesterday. Bob, the news director, told me."

"That Texas *gringo*," Aunt Alicia spits out.

"Bob could not have been kinder. And Aunt Alicia, and everyone, I'm going to be fine. I've already been contacted by another station, but I can't say anything, and you can't either. All this was supposed to be announced tomorrow. I don't know who spoke to the newspaper, but I came down as soon as I saw it because I knew you'd all be upset, because you're all so kind and hardworking. And you should not blame Lizzie, because Bob told me she didn't know and I believe her, and she's a doll."

Alicia is tearing up now, but she takes my hand. What a wonderful person, to worry about the Help Center and me.

Aunt Alicia is still rumbling, "What kind of sister don't know what the other sister—"

"Tia Alicia," her niece hushes her gently, and then with a forced smile, repeats to us all, "Really, I'm going to be fine."

We all applaud. Nick helps me take the *Congratulations Help Center* birthday cake out of its box. We all beg Alicia to cut it and eat the first slice. It's only 10:30 in the morning, but we sense today is not going to get any more festive. Everyone hugs and kisses

Alicia, especially me. Nick hasn't said anything, but he kisses Alicia's hand.

The volunteers resume answering calls. I go into my office and cry for this lovely young woman, and a little bit for me.

29

NICK

"Let's stretch our legs. I could use some fresh air." Bob Beardsley is leading me out through the studio to the back of the weather wall, where there's a door to the patio that faces Biscayne Bay.

After the gloom, not only of the darkened studio, but of the newsroom as well, which seems like a funeral home, it's blinding to step outside. The patio has a permanent camera positioned on a canopy. Out of camera view, there are three round tables with umbrellas. Wonder why Lizzie and I have never brought lunch here? Speedboats are making waves. Sailboats are lolling in the sun. You can see the long causeway to Key Biscayne. Lizzie's building is blocked by taller ones to our right.

Bob says nothing. He's good at that, having once told Lizzie, *"When you're quiet, people think you know more than you do."* Don't know if he was commenting on his own silence or Lizzie's gushing, which I love. But I'm often quiet, too, and people think it's arrogant or aloof. You never get that sense from this almost cadaverously lean man next to me, with his white pompadour and electric blue eyes. He's as calm as a Texas prairie before a storm.

"Look, Bob," I begin, "I'm not an employee here."

"Still part of the family."

"And you must be up to your neck in questions about—"

"This goddamn mess. Aunt Alicia didn't have questions. I thought she was going to skin me. But I'm glad you came to my office. Because I knew Lizzie wouldn't't."

"She's not mad at you," I say.

"I know. She's got common sense. But she also has pride, which I like."

We walk down steps and through a gate for the WTAN building that's closed to the public. Now we're on a public walkway along the bay. It's a weekday and we're in the business end of Brickell, so there aren't many people here.

"Has Lizzie spoken with Karen?" Bob doesn't look at me.

"We found out when Aunt Alicia showed us the newspaper. Do you know who spoke to the paper?"

"I have suspicions. Is Lizzie close to her sister? I know they didn't speak after the *Backstory…*"

After Bob lets it hang, and shrugs, I complete his sentence, "Blow up."

He doesn't smile. I wasn't trying to make a joke. When I'm with Bob, I get as laconic as he is.

We walk in silence for a while longer. Girls on a boat with a lime green sail wave to us. We wave back, Bob bigger than I would've guessed. Public relations and Texas geniality. He's in shirtsleeves with a skinny blue tie. I'm not wearing a tie.

After a moment, he drawls, "I hear you used to know Karen."

By now, I assume Bob knows plenty about everything.

"Back in college," I say.

"This going to be complicated for you?"

"No," I say.

I was going to ask, why? or what do you mean? But this is Bob, so I say no and leave it at that. And he knows I don't mean it.

By now, I think I have the right to ask, "Was this your decision?"

He says nothing for a while, probably to let it sink in that my question is impertinent.

But then he says, "No."

He doesn't bother to say, keep this to yourself or only tell Lizzie. Bob seems to know I'll keep it between Lizzie and myself.

So he explains, "Sheryl MacDonald's being replaced as head of UBN News by Fred Arhaus. You probably don't know him."

"No."

We sit on a bench.

"I don't know him, either. And by the way, I don't know Karen Lomax. Saw her once at a corporate get-together. She seemed pleasant. Everyone does. Anyway, the network's big beef against MacDonald was that she took her eye off things like *Backstory* because she was micromanaging the O and O's. The guy who objected to that most was, of course, Steve Rosser. He's supposed to manage the O and O's. He still does. In fact, he will now more than ever."

Bob pauses to let this sink in or to catch his breath. I've never heard him talk this much before.

"I mention all this," Bob resumes, "because I want you to warn Lizzie that Rosser is no fan of hers. Not because of anything she's done. Lizzie's great. You know that. Rosser doesn't like that Sheryl MacDonald pushed her. And of course, that MacDonald countermanded him about Lizzie sitting on the desk."

"So is Rosser—"

Bob interrupts, which he never does. "I don't know what he's going to do. We're not buddies, either. But Lizzie's been sideswiped by an awful lot lately." He gets up and I follow. "And I don't want her to be shocked again."

We walk back toward the station.

Then Bob asks, "You two casual or what?"

Normally, I'd resent the question, but I don't from him.

"She's coming to my mom's place for Thanksgiving tomorrow because you made her work. Otherwise, she'd be with her family in New York."

Bob lets that pass. "She'll be anchoring tomorrow morning. That's something."

"Yes, it is. And she's grateful."

Bob pulls a bag of peanuts out of his pocket. So he does eat something. He holds out the bag. I start to refuse but realize this is hospitality. Maybe even friendship.

Sure enough, Bob changes the subject. Or does he?

"My wife, Jan, married me when I was on the assignment desk in San Antonio, making twelve thousand dollars a year. She was waiting tables. Then she got into an accident. A kid hit her. Had his license two weeks. He was okay, but Jan hurt her back. The good thing that came out of it was acupuncture. Jan got some, and she learned it. Soon, she was making more than I did. And she's been able to do it from home wherever we've gone. Wherever we go is home, even if it's not Texas. Because Jan was there with the kids. And now grandkids, when they visit. We're married forty-two years."

"Congratulations."

"Indeed," Bob replies. And he offers me more peanuts.

<u>30</u>

NICK

It's 6 a.m. and I'm sitting up in bed at my place, watching Lizzie on the morning show warn about a storm off Martinique and Saint Lucia. She's measured and authoritative, as they say. So is Valerie, the morning meteorologist, without any melodrama. I don't know if Lizzie's roommate Meg is on a cruise heading that way and if it'll have to be diverted, but I hope she's okay. No rain here yet, so I'm still hoping to take the boat out tonight with Lizzie after Thanksgiving.

"We'll be keeping an eye throughout the morning on Tropical Storm Ellis," Lizzie says. *"And let's hope it doesn't turn into anything worse. Meantime, is there a storm brewing in your oven?"*

Ouch. Well, television news writing has its own rules. They include unfunny puns, labored segues, like that one, from one story to the next, and making sure every dream turns into a nightmare.

Lizzie's reading scripts. And this being her first time anchoring here, I doubt that she suggested any changes. Whatever the words are, she's moving effortlessly from one emotion to the next and—really, no special pleading here—she's delightful.

The phone rings.

"Are you watching this, man?" It's Harry.

Another voice talks over him, "Is she or is she not fucking brilliant? Pure sunshine. Apart from the storm."

"That's exactly what I was thinking, Ardis."

Apparently she grabbed Harry's phone, since I hear her more clearly now. In fact, I have to hold my phone away from my ear.

"All right, hang up," Ardis orders. "I want to see these tips about cooking a turkey."

"You're not cooking." Harry laughs from the background.

"Not this year, but—okay, gotta go."

And they're gone. Ardis will be feasting with Harry's mom, up in Jupiter. That's a long drive, so I hope she's grown to like his Hummer, especially after Harry put in new shocks and a comfy seat cushion.

I put off the morning run 'til seven, when the network morning show starts and Lizzie only cuts in for news headlines near the top and bottom of each hour. But hell, I don't want to miss a minute of her, so I'll go out at nine.

That's my girlfriend. And she's brilliant.

***

LIZZIE

As always, Nick opens the passenger door. I hand him the pie and swivel out, keeping my knees together the way Duchess Meghan would, in case anyone's watching. This isn't hard, since the frock Ardis picked out from Bermuda Blues is almost ankle length. It's a russet-patterned garden dress that looks vintage. A hat would've been too much, but I think it calls for a hat. Maybe for Easter.

The pie is a gift from my Meg before she sailed. She said the ship's baker was making a bunch of pumpkin pies for friends and he'd be delighted to include one for the Harris family. So that's what I've brought.

"Tell her you baked it yourself," Meg urged.

This is shocking, because Meg never lies. I suppose she thinks it's okay for me to lie, which isn't really a compliment. I don't lie. Much. And never about anything serious. Anyway, I told Meg that Judge Harris would be equally impressed that I have a friend who went to the trouble of providing this pie. Meg's family, by the way, is joining her on this five-night Thanksgiving cruise. Ardis and I have standing invitations to visit them in Wisconsin. Since Ardis— like most Brits, I gather—is a fiend for cheese, Meg's family better store up.

Nick hands me the pie so I can present it. We walk around the circular driveway, already ringed with cars, and approach the front of his mother's house. Oh. My. God. It's the most magnificent home

I have ever seen. And Nick told me the best part is the back, facing the water. That's not possible. Spanish? Mediterranean? I don't have the architectural vocabulary to think of a good description. Suffice to say, if they made a movie called *Honey, I Shrunk the Biltmore*, it would be about this house.

As we approach, I expect next to see a liveried butler. Instead, the enormous wood and black iron door swings open without a creak and Judge Judith Harris welcomes us with open arms and the widest smile you can imagine. She wears glasses, a red top and white pants, and manages to embrace both Nick and me.

"Lizzie. I am so glad to see you. Oh, no, I'm crushing the pie. Is this a pie or a cake?"

"Pumpkin pie."

"My favorite. And not just for Thanksgiving. Here, give me that. Don't you look lovely."

Judge Harris has unabashed graying hair and a funny way of shaking her head when she speaks. Not funny, I bet, when she's sentencing you.

Now she steps back and surveys me. "This is not what you were wearing this morning."

"No, I changed."

"You were marvelous. So natural. Was that really your first time anchoring?"

"I filled in a couple times in Dayton. They couldn't run me out of town soon enough."

"I can't believe that." Judge Harris purses her lips, taking my arm with her free one and leading us inside.

On the way in, Nick gives her a quick peck on the cheek.

The suits of armor must be at the iron works being polished. That's how grand the entrance hall looks. But instead of paintings with attached overhead lights, the hall is covered with family photos reaching back, I'd guess, four or five generations. And lots of little Nick. Judge Harris sees me looking and offers a tour, not of the house, but of her family.

"This is Nick getting his first haircut. For a while, in college when I wasn't around, he let it grow longer than mine."

I laugh. "I saw his Vanderbilt yearbook."

"Wasn't that awful? We tried recalling all the books, but everyone else looked nice and ready to conquer the world. These are my parents."

It's their wedding photo. Her dad's in uniform. World War Two?

The judge continues, "You'll meet my mom in a moment. My father passed, oh… it's almost ten years now."

"Eleven," Nick says. The stickler.

Judge Harris shakes her head, slowly. "Mom's been alone eleven years."

"Not alone." Nick's arm is around his mom's shoulder.

"And you'll see, Lizzie, she's going a little downhill. Alzheimer's.

"Oh, I'm sorry."

"But she's still great. And this is my older brother, Marty, and his wife, Sue."

They're laughing on a boat with Judge Harris and Nick when he was about ten, and another boy a few years older.

Judge Harris continues quickly with her grandparents and great-grandparents until the woman I recognize from the photo as Aunt Sue joins us from a room on the left.

"What," she says, "you're ashamed to let her meet the rest of the family?" Aunt Sue kisses me and looks at the wall. "I look better now than in that picture. Now I'm a blonde."

We all laugh.

Aunt Sue tells me, "You were fabulous this morning. And both of you at the Help Center. I would volunteer, but Marty needs all my help at home. Come, say hello to him and Nick's cousin, Howard."

We walk past a library that looks like the J.P. Morgan Library in New York, where Mom got to see an actual Jane Austen manuscript. Judge Harris has her library decorated with flowers.

The crowd noise from a football game lures us into a relatively small sitting room with a TV, not as big as Nick's, but big enough.

Uncle Marty is yelling at the screen and at Howard. "What did I tell you? Amari Cooper's the man. Didn't I tell you?"

Aunt Sue says, "Marty, turn it down. Look who's here. From the Help Center."

Cousin Howard jumps up and gives Nick a guy hug. Uncle Marty looks around, sees me, and lifts himself to his feet. I spot a walker in the corner.

"Hello," he shouts. "So you're the gal who made my nephew a star."

I go over to shake hands. Marty hugs me, a big hug.

I say, "Nick didn't need any help from me. Not like the Cowboys needed Amari Cooper."

Marty, Nick, and Howard all marvel together, "You like football?"

"If I wanted to talk to my dad five months of the year, I had to *love* football."

"Sit down with us," they all shout, clearing space on the couch.

"Let Dallas finally make it to the Super Bowl and Lizzie can come back," Judge Harris says. And then to me, "When you're a single mom, you learn to like everything. And I hope you come back sooner than that."

So Nick plops down with his uncle and cousin, and his mom and Aunt Sue muscle me toward the kitchen.

On the way I say, sincerely, "Judge Harris, I have never seen a home so warm and beautiful."

"Warm is more important than beautiful."

"And she's not saying that," Aunt Sue jokes, "because you're beautiful and I'm warm."

The girls laugh until the judge chides me, "What is this *Judge Harris* nonsense? Have you committed some crime we don't know about? Call me Judy. And when you meet Mom, call her Mom. That's all she responds to, when she does."

The kitchen is big enough for Meg's cruise ship. Spanish tiles color the floor and the walls. A small older lady they introduce as Marianna is checking on the turkey. The even older lady at the table in the corner, looking forlornly out the window, is Judy and Marty's mother.

"Doesn't that smell fabulous, Mom?" Aunt Sue gives her a kiss. "How about a round of applause for Marianna?"

Sue, Judy, and I clap. Marianna laughs. Grandma stares out the window. Judy doesn't introduce me and I know that's because Grandma would only be confused. I have one grandparent left, but we're lucky. Nanna Nelson, Mom's mother, is still the life of the party.

***

NICK

Lizzie told me she tried calling Karen yesterday, after we found out about her coming to Miami. Her sister still hasn't called back or left a text or an email. Their parents are with Karen in New York. Lizzie hasn't wanted to go around Karen and call them. But now, as we're sitting in Mom's courtyard, amazed as I always am by the tropical flowers and the water, and now by Lizzie, her phone rings. Lizzie sees the number and gets up to excuse herself, saying it's her mother, but my mother asks if she can say hello. Mom isn't pushy. I haven't met Lizzie's family yet, except for Karen. But I suspect Mom wants them to know how welcome their daughter is here. And I appreciate that. Hope Lizzie does, too.

"Hello, Mom. Happy Thanksgiving. I want to hear everything, but Judge Harris—Nick's mom—wants to say hello. Yes. Here she is."

Mom takes the phone. "Hello, Mrs. Lomax? Cindy, thank you. And please call me Judy. Yes, Judge Judy." Mom laughs as though she hasn't heard this a million times before. "I don't want to keep you. May I say thank you for sharing your wonderful daughter. We saw her this morning anchoring the morning show. And of course, we see her on the news all the time with Nick. Thank you, Cindy. And Nick's a good guy, which is more important. I want to tell you what a terrific job you've done with Lizzie, and to wish you a joyful, happy Thanksgiving. Yes, I hope so, too. I really do. Thank you, Cindy. My best to your family. Here's your daughter."

Mom gives the phone back to Lizzie, who disappears inside the house. Uncle Marty and Howie have now joined us in the courtyard as we wait for Marianna to call everyone in. She's been with us all my life, and I hope she'll join us for a toast. Mom always asks Marianna to leave the kitchen without cleaning up so she can enjoy Thanksgiving with her own family.

"How old are you, Nicky?" Uncle Marty asks, out of the blue.

I tell him, twenty-nine.

"It's the thing now for your generation to wait 'til they're thirty-five or forty, or maybe never to settle down and start a family, right?"

"This is about me, Nick, not you." Howie laughs, uncomfortably.

"It's about both of you," Uncle Marty says.

For once, Aunt Sue doesn't shush him. He is the head of the family, and more important, she agrees.

"This girl," he looks me in the eye, "is a keeper."

"We've known each other only a couple months."

"So take it slow. But I'm telling you, don't let her get away."

"*Oh, no, they can't take that away from me,*" Grandma sings.

She has a surprisingly strong voice, and I like her taste in songs.

"Beautiful, Mom," my mother says.

Grandma sighs back into silence.

"Do you still write songs?" Aunt Sue asks me.

"Not often." I pretty much stopped after college.

"Well, if this girl can't inspire you," Uncle Marty says, "I don't know what will."

"You really like this girl, huh, Marty?" Aunt Sue winks at me. "Because when dinner's over, and if there's not another game on, Nick's boat is right there. I'm sure he won't mind if you two take off."

Mom says, "After you clean the dishes."

***

LIZZIE

A feast, indeed. I wanted at least two helpings of everything, especially the sweet potato casserole topped with melted marshmallows. But self-respect and my dainty dress dictated restraint. Speaking of the dress, Grandma, at one point, surprised everyone by saying she has a dress just like it. I think she meant in the past, but she could wear it now. Grandma's girlishly slender. Judy patted her mom on the hand.

With six people clearing, washing, and drying, cleaning up took no time at all. Uncle Marty and Howie returned to the Cowboys and Redskins. Aunt Sue is taking a walk with Nick. Judy and I are relaxing on chaise lounges facing Indian Creek, right across from the Fontainebleau, praying that digestion will help us atone for gluttony.

The sun is setting. The sky is still clear. I thanked Judy and she thanked me for coming, so we're past all that. We've reached the stage where we can sit quietly.

Finally, I ask, "When did he start wearing bowties?"

Judy chuckles. "They make too much about that. Nick's not really so formal. As a teenager, he saw Indiana Jones wearing a bow tie in a classroom and all the girls he was teaching swooned over him. That's the story. Nick was crazy about girls." She paused. "And he's a little bit formal. He likes to be a contrarian."

I think about that. "Why?"

She lets out a breath. "Well, you know he hasn't seen his father since he was nine."

"Yes."

"Does he talk about that?"

"No."

Judy looks at me. "It's not because he's keeping something from you or he doesn't care for you. Do you mind my saying? I think he does care about you. You're the first girl, the first young woman he's brought to the house in I don't know how long. And it's not because you're colleagues. Is he nice to work with?"

"Yes. The volunteers love him. And the people in the stories. You've seen."

"Yes." His mother smiles. "That lady in Overtown. That's the Fontainebleau right there. And the Eden Roc next to it. When that lady talked about how Nat King Cole wasn't allowed to stay at Miami Beach hotels, it's that kind of thing that made me want to become a judge."

"After your husband..." I don't know how to end. Does Judy mind my asking?

She takes a deep breath and a sip of the white wine on the table between us. "My ex-husband comes from a prominent family. His great-grandfather went in with Collins, Pancoast, and Fisher."

The Collins Avenue Collins?" I ask.

"And the Fisher Island Fisher. He invested with them and," Judy points to the hotels again, "there's the result." She sits up and looks at me. "My father was no slouch, either. He was Miami's most prominent cardiologist. There's a wing at Jackson Memorial named after him. So I didn't go into my marriage with hat in hand. But I was naïve. I didn't know that my husband liked young girls. Very young girls."

I blink.

Judy's still looking at me. "I'm not telling you anything that's not common knowledge. Particularly after my ex-husband was back in the news years ago for taking a senator and a former president down to a private island to have sex with teenagers. That happened after he left me, when Nick was in college. Didn't your sister ever mention it?"

"No."

"Well," Judy pours us both more wine, "maybe she was trying to protect Nick. I'd like to think so."

We both drink. An evening tour boat is pulling out from a marina.

"The tourists on that boat want to see all the beautiful houses," Judy says. "But what goes on in these houses is not always beautiful. So there I was. Thirty years old. Harvey left me quite comfortable, as we say, with a settlement and alimony and this house. And the chance to go to law school. And a little boy who had no idea why his father was too ashamed to have anything to do with him. Anything, Lizzie. Not a visit. Not a call. Not a birthday card. Nothing.

"As far as I know, since he's grown up, Nick has never reached out to his father. He went through a James Bond phase and an Indiana Jones phase. You can still see the traces. He wrote songs that his friend Harry—you know Harry? Yes, I'm sorry, I forgot. Next time, Sue and I have to go with you to LIV. Anyway, Nick and Harry still watch games and take the boat out. My son is a loyal friend."

"That's why I always wondered what happened between Nick and Karen."

His mom pauses and then looks at me again. "You know, there was never anything serious between them. He never brought her home."

I take that in and smile.

She continues, "Tell him what we talked about, if you like. I don't keep secrets from Nick. But maybe better if you wait for him to bring it up about his father. If he does."

"I think you're right."

"You must come from a nice family," Judy says. "Wasn't your father shot once? When Nick knew Karen in college?"

"Yes," I say. "My father is wonderful. He's fine now. And he loves my mother very much." Maybe I shouldn't have said that.

But Judy smiles, ruefully. "So at least one of you had a normal home."

"I think we both have normal homes. We both have the best mothers."

And she pats my hand.

***

NICK

This is the best Thanksgiving I've ever had. Lizzie and I are now out on my boat. She's loving it and I do, too. We steer into Biscayne Bay. Then we'll pass WTAN and then her apartment. It's a clear night. The stars will be beautiful, and not a shark in sight.

***

LIZZIE

Nick's boat isn't a cabin cruiser, like Joel's. There's nowhere to sleep unless you scrunch down on the deck. My dress is demure, but not when it's folded up. There's only one thing to do to avoid getting seasick. And we're doing it.

<u>31</u>

NICK

Sunday night, my cell rings. The name on the screen is Karen. That could be anyone, but it's not.

"Hello," I say, in a neutral voice.

"Hi, stranger."

"Hi. Lizzie's not here."

Why did I say that? Because when I'm caught off guard, I revert to being rude? To let her know Lizzie's the only Lomax I care to hear from?

"I know," Karen says. "We just spoke."

"And she gave you my number?"

"No. Steve Rosser did."

"I don't know how he—"

"He thought we ought to get reacquainted, Nick. Not that I think we could ever be strangers."

"Look, Karen—"

"I have your address, too, but I didn't want to show up at your door."

"Thank you for that."

"I'll be there in twenty—the driver says twenty-five minutes."

"I'm going out."

Karen laughs. "No you're not, Nick. I love that you're still such a terrible liar."

She disconnects.

I walk out onto the balcony. It's getting dark. The ocean's losing its definition again. Lizzie is back at her place and I should call her, but I don't.

***

LIZZIE

This is how it's going to be? Karen flies down without telling me. She lands at Miami International at two in the afternoon, when I would have been delighted to pick her up, though it would've meant borrowing Ardis's car again. But Karen doesn't ask me to get her. She doesn't call me until—what is it now—9:15 p.m. And she doesn't want me to come to her hotel. She'll see me tomorrow at the station. I feel like calling Mom. Then I feel like calling Nick. But Mom would say we have to cut Karen a lot of slack, with all that she's going through. And while I always want to talk with Nick, I don't want to talk with him about Karen.

Thankfully, Meg sailed home today. I'm a bad influence, since she usually wants to go on a crash diet after a cruise, but I'll talk her into splitting a half-gallon of Ben & Jerry's Chunky Monkey. Then nobody will try squeezing me into a micro-mini.

***

NICK

Karen Lomax will be here in twenty minutes. Eight years ago, I called Karen twenty times, hoping against hope, not that she would come back to me, but that she would let me come see her. It took years to stop hoping, and the only thing that finally made me forget Karen, or at least give up, was watching her grow more and more successful, more and more famous, until the idea that she'd ever want to see me again was a joke.

Hey, I'm not asking you to feel bad for me. I'm the luckiest guy in the world. Good job, wonderful family, great friends, and the nicer and lovelier of the Lomax sisters is my girlfriend. Is that why Karen called? No. Lizzie told her sister about me weeks ago and Karen couldn't have cared less. Which was fine. So is it simply that network star Karen Lomax is coming to work at a local station in Miami, alongside the sister she left behind long ago, and that Karen doesn't want some old boyfriend making her feel even worse?

I'm still in my gym clothes and actually do start to go out again, to resume the run that ended right before Karen called. Then I realize how juvenile that would be. Instead, I consider changing into better clothes, and then think the hell with that. Then, as I'm about to do what I should've done twenty minutes ago—call Lizzie—the buzzer sounds and Henry says Karen Lomax is downstairs.

"Please tell her I'll be right down." There's no way she's coming up here.

Call Lizzie? I will, but why upset her before I know what her sister wants. Maybe Lizzie already knows. I walk to the elevator, and the only concession I've made to impressing Karen Lomax is pulling on a clean shirt with a WTAN logo.

She's appraising a splashy abstract painting in the lobby, shaking her head as though it's not worth much. Karen, of course, looks like a million dollars. She didn't wear this silky floral dress and platform heels to fly down in, even first-class, so what I assume is a pretty chic ensemble must be for my benefit.

"I appear to be underdressed," I say.

She turns and appraises me. "You always looked good underdressed." And Karen steps in to kiss me.

I give her my cheek and make no move to reciprocate. "Good flight?"

"Under the circumstances," she says, wryly, raising her eyebrows.

Have to give Karen credit. She never pulled any punches.

"That's what I'd like to talk about, Nick, after we catch up." She starts toward the elevator. "Can we go up to your place? I want to see if you still wallow on a waterbed."

"It's a warm night," I deflect. "There's a boardwalk behind the building. You must want to stretch your legs, after two hours on a plane."

"Great. Maybe we can even dip our toes in the ocean."

This is a more frolicsome Karen than I remember. Determined to be happy.

A walkway leads directly to the boardwalk. We head in the direction of the Fontainebleau and LIV. I figure that'll keep me focused. For a while, Karen silently breathes in the briny sea air and lets the rhythm of the waves dictate our pace.

Then she asks, "Where's your famous Moon Over Miami?"

I point to the silver fluorescence of a cloud the moon is hiding behind.

"Oh," Karen says. "I hope it comes out soon."

Because I live so near and go there often, the guards at the Fontainebleau know me, and we could go to the bar by the pool for a drink. Karen probably expects that, maybe needs one. Instead, I turn around and we retrace our steps. Halfway back to my place, she points out a bench and asks if we can sit and talk. A couple close to the water appears to be making love.

"Look at that." Karen laughs. "Are they remaking *From Here to Eternity*?" You know, the scene where waves crash over Burt Lancaster and Deborah Kerr.

"The X-rated version, maybe." I'm not laughing.

Sometimes kids are around, and it's not funny.

"Let's move down to that bench." Karen points. "I've seen enough."

I look her in the eyes, really for the first time. "So have I."

"Well, that's not a great way to begin a relationship. Even a working relationship."

"I work for the attorney general."

"You've been working closely with Lizzie."

"That's true."

We reach the next bench and sit.

"Did she enjoy Thanksgiving with your family?"

"I hope so. How was your Thanksgiving? Has your father been well?"

"Well? Oh."

What the hell. Let's have this out.

"I mean, is he fully recovered, Karen? Doesn't it seem like only yesterday that you had to run home to be with your father in the hospital? And you wouldn't let me drive you, or tell me how he was or anything. We're talking now more than we did then."

"Are you still angry?"

Am I? "Of course."

"I was wrong."

"You were embarrassed."

"Embarrassed?" And for a moment, she's off-balance.

"Yes. I didn't realize it then, but I get it now. Because being here is all about being embarrassed, isn't it? You never told me before that night that your father was a police officer. Like that was something to be ashamed of. Then you had to explain because I was standing right there with you in the hotel. What did you tell the girls at Kappa? Did you speak to them at all? Barbara said you never came back. I would've loved to come with you to Cincinnati, to meet your father and mother and sister, to help any way I could. To show them I cared. I thought we were in love, Karen. And that we might have a future."

"You had no idea what you wanted to do."

That stops me. "No, I didn't. And now, what am I? An assistant in the Florida AG's office, assigned to do consumer reports."

"You could still do anything. With your education, and looks, and background."

"My background is crap. I don't mean my mother, but…" I take a breath and stare at the ocean, which is disappearing in the dark except for the sound that seems fainter and fainter. "Look, Karen," but I don't look at her, I'm looking at Lizzie, "everything's worked out for the best."

And we sit in not so companionable silence.

"Was there a bar at that hotel?" she finally asks.

"Yeah," I say, knowing I've been acting boorishly. And recalling a happier time, "Still like Hpnotiq?"

"What," she snaps.

That's a blue liqueur Karen drank whenever she could back in college, I think because it came from France. Now she sounds defensive.

"Just kidding," I say.

"Are you still chugging iced tea?"

"You bet."

Karen gets up, begins to walk back to the hotel, and then stops. The moon is now out, making her look like a silhouette.

"Listen," she says, "I didn't come to reminisce. There's something I need to tell you before showing up at the station tomorrow."

"What?"

She leans on the boardwalk's wooden rail and faces the sea.

I ask, "Does Lizzie know? What you need to tell me?"

"No."

Silence.

"Is she going to like it?"

Karen turns and forces a smile. "I think she will. It's going to be good for everyone. I mean, this whole mess, the Luxor mess, is going to make things sticky at first."

"A sticky mess? That's how you see it?"

"I'm not going to explain to you how I see it," she flares up. "I don't have to defend myself to *you*."

And now it all comes back. What I knew and what I didn't want to know. This is the Karen who turned on me at the Hermitage Hotel. Who turned on the stone staircase she tripped on at the Parthenon, for crying out loud, and anything else that dared get in her way. And now I see, finally, that I never meant anything to her.

"It's going to be sticky," she quickly calms down, "in public. People are still throwing stones nationally." She laughs, dismissively. "And I understand the paper here has a gossip columnist who writes every day about local anchors, and even reporters."

"Even reporters," I repeat. "Like Lizzie."

"They didn't care about that in Houston, much less New York."

"Well, you're not in New York anymore, Karen. Local TV means more here, in the sticks."

"Miami is not the sticks. Steve Rosser didn't send me to the sticks. I'm here to show that without stupid producers out to make a name for themselves, I can do investigative reporting on my own. That's what got me to the network, and that's what's going to get me back."

"How are you going to prove that as an anchor?" I ask in a harsh tone. "Sitting behind a desk and reading scripts? I like John McIntyre, but no one thinks he's an investigative journalist."

"We met once, a few years ago." Karen shakes her head again. "In LA, covering the Oscars. Talk about old school. McIntyre expected the emcee to be Bob Hope."

"So you're going to do investigations. And you need to tell me about it?"

I'm getting a glimmer about why she needs to talk. And I'd better be wrong. Is it worth pumping Karen to find out? And then what? What can we do tonight, if I'm right? This stinks. If I'm right, she stinks.

"It's late, Karen. Go get your beauty sleep. Lizzie and I will see you tomorrow."

We walk back. Henry calls a cab for Karen. I return to the boardwalk and run until I'm ready to drop.

32

NICK

In the past, I've shown up on my own for these station meetings. As Bob Beardsley said, I am part of the family. This time, I got a call from the general manager's assistant, asking me to come. We're back on folding chairs in the studio, pretty much the entire staff. The meeting is catered. Pizza, vegetables, cake, and beverages. Yet nobody's eating much.

Word's gone around that Karen is here. I haven't sought her out. I sit next to Lizzie. She didn't want me to pick her up this morning, saying the walk would do her good. I sense that—either because Karen told her or because Lizzie is smarter than both of us—she's already figured things out. But she betrays nothing and sits with me, along with most of the Help Center volunteers, who are eager to see Karen. Aunt Alicia isn't one of them. She quit when her niece was fired.

When we're all seated, Doug Long, the GM, walks in, followed by Karen and two men I don't know. In a business suit, Karen looks even more remarkable. Not as beautiful as Lizzie, inside or out. But the times I've gotten to meet a few famous people, I've noticed that they look different. Partly it's the aura from that fame. Partly, when they're in entertainment or even politics, it's a kind of buffed and tailored quality. That's Karen. Nothing flashy, but perfect in a blue suit and heels that easily put her at eye level with all three men. She smiles, yet I think everyone can sense she's nervous. Or embarrassed.

Doug Long takes a hand-held mic. The lights slowly dim except for one on him, and the studio screens come to life. They flash the UBN and WTAN logos against a Miami panorama. He begins.

"First, congratulations on a great book." The screens now show the November ratings of each Miami station. "We decisively finished ahead of everyone except the bad guys at that scare-tactic station." He points to the screen. "Booo."

We all join in booing. It's like Orwell's *Nineteen Eighty-Four*, though more good-natured.

"But, gang, they're now sweating," Doug Long continues, "because, look at that, we're right on their heels. So give yourselves a big round of applause."

Everyone claps, enthusiastically. Long goes on to praise the sales and promotion departments. Then he mentions how the new satellite truck and other equipment helped get the jump on the competition. And he thanks Fred Arhaus, the new head of UBN News—Sheryl MacDonald's successor—who's now formally introduced. Long notes that it's a big deal to have the news head visiting, and says we're the first O and O outside New York to get him. We all seem impressed.

Arhaus takes the mic. He's completely bald and wears glasses with stylish thick black frames. Arhaus himself is thicker than I expect a New York honcho to be, but his manner is sleek, assured, and jovial.

"Where else did you expect me to visit when I escape from a New York snowstorm? Denver?"

We all laugh. He adds to Doug Long's congratulations, praises several of the department heads, and for the first time I notice that Bob Beardsley isn't up front. I don't see him anywhere.

Fred Arhaus then introduces the man I've heard too much about. The man who hired Harry Lutz to pose women on desks, and who didn't want Lizzie to head the Help Center. I'm unobtrusively holding her hand. It tightens as Steve Rosser takes the mic. He's about the same age as John McIntyre and used to be an anchor, too, though unlike John he never made it to any big markets—at least not as an anchor. As a manager and executive, this generically handsome guy with a deep, professionally modulated voice is now second-in-command at UBN News. And from what Bob Beardsley told me, Steve Rosser has a free hand for the first time.

"Unlike Fred," he booms, "it's my job to visit the O and O's, and there's no UBN station that it's more of a pleasure to see grow and prosper than WTAN. Fred's never seen this new studio before. Not bad, eh?"

Arhaus gives a thumbs up. The control room sets the giant screens flashing like someone just won a Vegas jackpot. Everyone laughs.

Rosser continues, "For many old-timers, like Lenny—stand up and take a bow, Lenny—it was hard to say goodbye to the old place, which was part of Miami history."

"I couldn't wait to say goodbye," Lenny pipes up. "That dump had rats."

Everyone laughs, even Lizzie.

"Well, I hope there are no rats here," Rosser jokes.

And no one laughs.

"It's also hard when the inevitable happens in this business. Someone moves on."

John McIntyre straightens up. Is Rosser talking about him?

"But one of the great things about being owned by a network is that we've got an incredibly deep bench. There aren't many towns that are big enough, exciting enough, glamorous enough to handle a network star. One who's not only glamorous, but also an award-winning war correspondent, and investigative journalist. I am not going to sugarcoat it. She wouldn't want me to. Karen Lomax got a bad break, through no fault of her own. But Miami can be grateful, because starting tonight, Karen Lomax joins Miami legend John McIntyre as the face and the journalistic standard for WMIA news."

Karen turns on a dazzling smile. She isn't going to speak. The applause is warm, if not enthusiastic. Alicia had many friends, but they know better than I that Rosser is right. It's a tough business. And I suspect it's about to get tougher.

***

LIZZIE

As we file out of the studio, Doug Long's assistant, Sheila, asks Nick and me to meet Doug in his office. It's on the second floor. I've been there only once, when Doug and Bob first told me about the Help Center. That was one of the happiest days of my life. This won't be.

The office is at the back of the building, looking out on Biscayne Bay. There aren't as many boats out today, the Monday after Thanksgiving, but Miami's never at a loss for people on holiday. Nick and I are the first to arrive. Doug and the others must be held up talking to people. Maybe it's a show of trust and friendliness that Sheila leaves us in Doug's office. We see local Emmy awards on the shelves. Pictures of the Long family with their four kids, all young in these photos. And floor-to-ceiling windows, with a sliding door leading to a private balcony.

Nick and I take two seats in front of Doug's desk, when the others enter in high spirits and all smile at me—Doug, Steve Rosser, and Karen. I saw Karen this morning, before the meeting. Big hug then. Jokes about Dad and *Hamilton*, which he liked more than I would've guessed, and the Macy's Thanksgiving Day Parade. Fred Arhaus isn't here. I understand that a meeting with me doesn't warrant his presence. He must be in the large conference room, making calls. Bob Beardsley isn't here, either.

Doug asks if we can all sit at the round table at the other end of his office. He introduces Nick to Rosser, who says nothing about Nick's work. Rosser may look like an anchorman, but Nick looks like a movie star. He's wearing a gray pinstripe suit and a long red tie. I can tell that Nick didn't want to advertise himself with his trademark bow tie.

Always affable, Doug looks at me and says, "Lizzie and Nick, and really Lucy should be here as well. We'll meet with her later when she can take a break from all the calls at the Help Center."

"Lucy is the best," I say.

"Yes, she is. Steve is eager to meet her."

We smile, a little. Rosser doesn't appear eager to meet any of us, apart from Karen.

But Doug redoubles, "We really should have acknowledged at the staff meeting how big a part the Help Center played in this month's ratings."

So it was Rosser who kept the Help Center from getting a round of applause.

"And not only the ratings," Doug insists. He stares at me, earnestly, worryingly. "Your Help Center has won us respect and friendship all throughout our community. You've done a remarkable job, Lizzie, getting it off the ground. And now," Doug looks away from me, down at his folded hands, "your reward. I saw you anchor Thanksgiving morning. I had hoped to sleep late, but Elyse banging around in the kitchen woke us all up." He laughs and we join him. "And I'm glad she did wake me, because Lizzie, you were excellent. I showed Steve some of the show before today's meeting. Wasn't she great?"

"Sure," Steve Rosser says, noncommittally, speaking for the first time. And then he smirks and looks me right in the eye. It's the creepiest look I've ever seen. "But we disagree, I'm afraid, about your taste in clothes."

After an awkward pause, Doug Long clears his throat. "Well, it confirmed what we had been thinking. A win-win. Karen cannot be confined to sitting behind an anchor desk. That's not who she is. She has to be out investigating. By the same token, Lizzie, you need to be behind an anchor desk, in addition to reporting. You both need to show Miami all you can do. What the Lomax sisters can do. It's a great opportunity. So Lizzie, we want you to join Carlos as our new "weekend"… morning anchor. And you'll join your sister Monday, Tuesday, and Wednesday nights—our prime nights because of football on Thursdays—as one of our lead reporters. General assignment reporters. You've earned it, and well, this is going to be great."

"But," Nick asks, "what about the Help Center?"

Rosser tilts his head, drops a pen he'd been toying with, and glances at Nick, dismissively. "The attorney general is still assigning you to the Help Center. And it's a perfect fit… for Karen. Now, with a star like Karen here, I want to see the stories get bigger, more important, especially for February sweeps. That means we've got to get started right away. Of course, with primary anchoring and appearances and everything else, Karen can't do all these investigations herself. Even with your assistance. So we're hiring a producer from Chicago, Deborah Canning."

"You'll love her," Doug gushes to Karen and Nick. "She's top-notch." He turns to me. "How many stories do you have in the can, Lizzie?"

For a moment, I have difficulty finding my voice. But I haven't looked angry or even disappointed. This is not a surprise. It could've been worse. I understand the way the station and the network see it, and they're lucky to have Karen. I'm lucky she's here, too. If it weren't for my sister, I bet Rosser—once they got rid of Sheryl MacDonald—would've kicked me out on my ass. Weekend morning anchoring in a market like Miami is pretty good at age twenty-five. All this is true.

But I'm crushed.

I smile. "We have stories ready to go for tonight and Wednesday."

"Lizzie, you've been super about keeping ahead of schedule," Doug says. "And we've got to keep that up. So here's what we're going to do. Let's hold both those stories. The Help Center is on vacation this week. Not the phones. We'll keep taking calls. But no stories this week. And Lizzie, you're getting five extra days of vacation. Take them starting today, before you start anchoring Saturday morning. You've earned it. Now, Karen and Nick." Doug pauses to take them in. "You two look great together. And we're going to roll you out, not on camera, but for all of Miami's movers and shakers tonight. The annual Beaux Arts Ball is tonight at the Lowe Art Museum, and Steve and I want you to go as a couple. Did you bring down something formal, Karen?"

"Always." She smiles. "I packed a bathing suit and a Valentino gown."

"And," Doug turns to him, "you have a tuxedo, don't you Nick?"

Karen laughs to the others. She's avoided looking at me. "The last time I saw Nick, back in college, he was wearing a tuxedo, and I bet you could still get into it."

"That's right." Doug grins. "Karen tells us you're old friends."

"Although," Karen says, "I'm sorry to admit that Nick and I spoke last night for the first time in, what was it, eight years? But it was like old times."

Pause. Everything.

They spoke last night?

***

NICK

The meeting lasts a few minutes longer and I barely hear a word. As we walk into the hallway, Karen asks if there's someplace she and her sister and I can talk. HR has a small conference room. Lizzie asks if we can borrow it. When the door closes, I speak first. To Lizzie.

"Karen called me last night. She got my number from Rosser. Then she showed up at my building. We took a walk on the boardwalk and your sister didn't say one word about the Help Center. I found out about all of this at the same time you did."

Karen begins, "Lizzie—"

I cut her off, "And it was not like old times, Karen. There are no old times."

"This is between my sister and me, Nick. And come to think of it, Karen, there's really nothing more to say. About any of this. It's business."

Karen takes her sister by the shoulders. "Are you upset, Lizzie? Morning anchoring is a good opportunity. At your age—"

"You were on your way from Houston to Iraq at my age, Kary. We're not on the same track and I understand that. As for you and Nick—"

"There is no Karen and me," I insist.

Lizzie looks at me blankly. "Nick, Karen is here to work with you, and this is about work. Period."

"Exactly," Karen says to me. And then to her sister, "After all, Lizzie, it's not like this was your life's work. The Help Center's been on for only one month."

***

LIZZIE

I say nothing.

So Nick says, "You don't understand, Karen. This is something we were building. I love working with Lizzie. Everyone loves her."

Now for the first time, maybe for the first time in my life, I'm looking at my sister and see her for who she really is. She looks away.

"Why did you call Nick last night? And then go see him?" I ask Karen. "You didn't pick up or return my calls in New York. You got down here yesterday and you didn't call me 'til last night. And said nothing, not a word about this. What is it that you had to say to Nick? Tell me."

Karen says nothing. Then, "I didn't know how you'd feel about everything, Lizzie. And I didn't want to take on both you and Nick at the same time. So I thought, if Steve Rosser is throwing us together, let me at least see how Nick feels."

"And how do you feel?" I ask him.

Nick looks into my eyes and takes my hand, and I can see he's ready to quit.

And for now, that's good enough.

"Don't say anything," I tell him. "And don't do anything. Not now. You owe it to your office. I owe it to the station not to embarrass them. They've been good to me."

"But sweetheart—"

"Not now. Please." And I squeeze his hand.

Sure, for a moment I wanted Nick to tell my sister to go to hell. And no, I don't want the two of them looking like two movie stars on the red carpet tonight at that ball. I can imagine the campaign the station is going to mount. Billboards, buses, the bi-planes you still see over Miami Beach with long banners streaming behind. It all makes sense. I have no right to complain. And I really don't feel like crying.

Look, if there's one thing the Help Center has taught me, along with all the other stories I've done—Mrs. Lewis facing discrimination, a mother fighting cancer, Emily drowning in the river, for God's sake—it's that my life is pretty damn good. And it still is.

But I do so wish that I didn't have to go back to living in my sister's shadow.

With the man I've fallen in love with standing right beside her.

33

LIZZIE

"If we're rocketing eighty miles an hour over the ocean," I warn, "one of us has to stay sober."

We're on our way to Key West. Ardis is driving her Mini Cooper. Meg is in the front passenger seat, and I'm squashed in the back of this trash compactor of a car that's the color of Pepto Bismol, which I crave at this moment more than life itself.

"Is this your paranoia about sharks again?" Ardis asks.

It's not only that. The narrow causeway connecting South Florida's middle keys to the lower ones has been featured in action movies where fighter jets shoot at trucks loaded with nuclear bombs. Add that image to sharks and Ardis's suicidal driving, and I insist on taking over the wheel.

We pull over at the shaggily thatched Sunset Grille and Raw Bar. Ardis downs her second key lime martini, while Meg and I devour the most scrumptious key lime pie. We summon the waiter with semaphore motions, for a second slice.

This is how I'm spending my five-day vacation. It's not that I'm avoiding Nick, but we both need a break. Too much upheaval and too much doubt. He's now going to work with Karen as closely as the two of us did. The guy who, two months ago, I saw drooling over her on the lobby TV. The guy Karen called as soon as she hit town, since there's no current guy to distract her.

The pie sugar high isn't doing it. Only my fear of turning her Mini into a submarine keeps me from guzzling what's left of Ardis's martini.

Like the true pal she pretends not to be, Ardis dropped everything when I came home with the Help Center news.

Thankfully, she has a long-suffering partner at the shop who's willing to go it alone 'til we get back. Meg is between cruises, so she was free, too. Meg's idea of taking a break from cruising is probably not driving over the ocean. But that's Meg, never a complaint. And she lets me eat most of her pie.

When I told the Help Center volunteers about this forced vacation, Matthew and Kevin arranged for us to stay at the home of a friend who's away, but apart from that, I don't know why we're heading all the way down to Key West. None of us is a big Ernest Hemingway fan. And Key West is probably no better than right here at the Sunset Grille, which has something that gladdens my heart, Cincinnati's favorite game—corn hole. The object is to toss a beanbag through a hole in a board about thirty feet away. This may not sound exciting, but it is if you're drunk. I'm not, but Ardis hit our waiter twice. He's bringing more pie anyway. I used to be a waitress at TGI Fridays. The memory of kid birthday parties still keeps me awake with cold sweats. Weekend morning anchoring sounds better and better. If only Nick weren't locked in a live truck with Karen.

We've timed things beautifully. The sun is setting as we leave the Sunset Grille and head south. I realize the real danger isn't fighter planes or sharks, but being distracted by this absolutely spectacular orange and scarlet panorama. Still, we make it to Little Duck Key and fill up the tank, when I see people cleaning out the convenience store. They're loading up with everything from water bottles to milk, batteries, and even propane tanks.

"What's going on?" I ask a frantic woman in an SUV heading north with her three kids and a poodle.

"They've upgraded Nyla to Cat three and it's racing in from the Bahamas."

In the news business, we live and die by the weather. But with all that's going on, I had tuned out. The last I heard about Nyla last week, she was a tropical depression stalled in the east Atlantic.

I tell Meg and Ardis, and then I phone the assignment desk. Dale puts me through to Bob Beardsley.

"Lizzie?"

"You're back," I say.

"Everyone's back for this, and I'm glad you called in. Where are you?"

"Little Duck Key."

"Great. Drive to Homestead. Are you alone?"

"Two girlfriends are with me."

"Let them drop you off. One minute." Bob tells someone, probably Dale, "Have Kevin go down to Homestead. The base. Lizzie's there, or she will be in..." Bob's back with me. "How long will it take you to get there? Should be a couple hours, but what's traffic like?"

I look at the northbound lanes of the causeway. They're twice as crowded as a few minutes ago, and soon may be bumper-to-bumper.

"Getting bad," I say.

"It'll get worse. Have your friends drop you off at Homestead Air Reserve Base, at the main gate. Kevin will be waiting. Then tell your friends to head as far away as they can. Cris and Val figure this thing's going to hit tonight, maybe right near the base."

"Got it. Glad you're back."

"You, too. Lizzie?"

"Yes."

"Take care of yourself."

"I will."

34

LIZZIE

Weather reports on the radio are conflicting. Maybe to combat complacency, the National Hurricane Center warns that Nyla could make landfall smack in the middle of downtown Miami. That's well north of where we'll be, and of course, much more heavily populated. Miami hasn't suffered a direct hit in I don't know how long. There have always been fears that the high-rises like ours are too high, too close to the water, and for all their flash, shoddily constructed. Too many Miami builders, like other people around here, think it's not cool or profitable to follow a code. So let's hope the Hurricane Center is wrong and Nyla spares downtown.

Selfishly, I want to be in the middle of the action, so I hope Cris and Val are right about Homestead. Bob must be covering all bases. But sending our best photog, Kevin, down here means Bob trusts our forecasters, too.

During the two-hour crawl to the Air Force base, all three of us call loved ones. My parents are pulling their hair out. I can't get through to Nick.

At last, there's Kevin's live truck. Wherever Nyla does hit hardest, we'll have to send the big satellite truck. But this will do for now. Nyla seems to be losing some strength, but the winds around here are picking up. Palm fronds and other branches are pelting the ground.

"Go, go, go." I hug and kiss the girls.

"What's the most important thing you want me to grab from the apartment?" Meg asks. "We have to pass it on the way to Harry."

Harry's mother invited Ardis and Meg to stay with her up in Jupiter. Now they need to get up there, and pray that Nyla doesn't turn right and whack the coast above Palm Beach.

"There's nothing, really," I say. All my nicest things, I stole from Ardis. "Is the shop going to be okay?"

Ardis says Kim, her partner, hasn't returned calls. "But we have heavy duty shutters. I'm more worried about a storm surge from the beach. And flooding. And I'm worried about you." Ardis gives me another hug and then shakes me in frustration. "Come with us. Screw this lousy job. They treat you like shit, and now you're going to risk your bloody life for them."

"No time to argue. Get going."

They do, waving 'til I lose sight.

It's 8:15 p.m. The skies aren't getting dark, they're pitch black—freaking malevolent. Kevin doesn't have his mast up to get off a live shot, so I assume the Air Force wants him to move on. I walk around to the driver's side of the van, pound on the door. It opens...

And there's Nick.

"What?" I'm not sure I said it. I don't think any sound came out.

Nick jumps down and holds me as though we're in the eye of the storm, the calm and peaceful and beautiful center where nothing can go wrong. We kiss. I stroke his neck. And after a decent interval, Kevin moves into the driver's seat. He'd been in the back of the truck, checking the electronics.

"There'll be a few consumers needing help tonight." He grins.

"Bob said it was all right for you to bring him?" I ask Kevin.

"Stowaway," Nick says. "Nobody knows yet. Maybe they'll never know, so keep it quiet."

"The station," I say, "has to deal with liability."

Nick turns to Kevin. "Look who's the lawyer now. Sweetheart, I signed a waiver when we started going out on Help Center stories. I've even got a press card. And Bob's not going to hassle Kevin. You're like his daughter and Kev is like his son."

"We better take off," Kevin orders. "The desk says there's a shelter two miles from here. They want us on right away."

Most of Homestead is not well-to-do. Along the route, we see modest homes mixed with trailer parks. We follow families making a caravan to the shelter. It's an elementary school. The rain that had been gentle and sporadic is now biblical. While Kevin prepares the truck to go live and Nick lays down cable, I walk into the lunchroom, where about a hundred people are now gathered. Older folks and parents huddle around radios. I don't see any TV sets, apart from phone screens. We still have Wi-Fi, for now. Some children are playing video games while the more boisterous ones play tag. The shelter's rolled out cots, but many people brought their own bedding.

I ask a woman named Mary Anne Davidson if she'll step outside with me, where we want to do our first live shot. There'll be time later to shoot inside the shelter. Mary Anne agrees. She's perhaps thirty-five and lives in a trailer with her eight-year-old son and a daughter who's five. I don't ask to put the kids on camera. We'll have time for that later, and Kevin has them on B-roll.

The signal's established. Kevin found my IFB in my desk at the Help Center. That's the earpiece, molded to fit my ear, which lets me hear what we're broadcasting as well as the director in the control room and anything the anchors want to ask. Karen is anchoring with John. This is her first night.

Pat Diaz is live now. He's on Miami Beach, not far from Nick's place. The waves are mounting and so are fears of a surge and a deluge. So far, the rain up there doesn't seem as bad as we have here.

Standing in front of the school, Mary Anne is wearing a raincoat, and Kevin brought a yellow slicker with a hat for me. Nick's holding a huge umbrella over us, which threatens to blow inside out or to lift him away like Mary Poppins. Which might not be a bad thing, since they've spotted him back in the control room.

"Is that Nick?" asks Dave, the director.

"Yeah," I reply. "He came on his own. Don't make a big thing about it."

"Have a nice date." Dave laughs.

We're still at the laughing stage of this storm. That's not going to last.

"You're next, after Cris," Dave says. "Tell Nick to step out of the shot."

He does. Cris says what I half-hoped and half-feared, that the storm's about to make landfall near Homestead. He doesn't take credit for being right, but the anchors will remind anyone who wasn't watching. Cris tosses to Karen and she's the ultimate pro, calm but forceful, compassionate without getting gooey. She begins.

"Cris and Val have been predicting for more than an hour that Nyla's going to do her worst where our service members do their best, near Homestead Air Reserve Base. And that's why we sent our best there... my sister, Lizzie Lomax. Liz, where exactly are you and how bad is it right now?"

I tell Karen and everyone watching that we're outside the shelter and that it's getting scary. I explain what precautions people are being told to take if they can't get to a shelter. Now I introduce Mary Anne, and the control room covers some of the live interview with video Kevin shot earlier. Mary Anne's great, but listening to her, I know where we have to go next.

Mary Anne tells me, *"A bus came to bring a bunch of us here to the school where my kids go, so they're pretty cool with it."*

I say, *"I saw them running around inside."*

"Yeah, it'll take more than a hurricane to make them sit still."

"We'll take everyone inside this shelter a little later to show how you're doing."

"We're doing fine," Mary Anne says. *"But there was one lady at the park, Mrs. Clayton, who didn't want to get on the bus. I guess the driver wasn't allowed to force her. But I'm a little worried about her. A lot worried."*

"Well, we'll go check on her, right away. And I'll take a look at your place, Mary Anne. Is it all locked up good and tight?"

Mary Anne shakes her head. *"Honey, if this hurricane hits my trailer, it might as well be a can of beans."*

"But at least you and the kids are safe here. Thank you, Mary Anne." I turn to the camera. *"Stay tuned and we'll go see Mrs. Clayton and try to persuade her to come to the shelter—as everyone around here should be doing. Karen."*

Karen says, *"Please tell Mary Anne and her children that they're in our prayers. And Liz, don't do anything foolish. Mom and Dad would never forgive me."*

"See you a little later, sis."

***

NICK

The Rolling Acres trailer park is right off U.S. 1, so the road's not closed, as most others are now. We check on Mary Anne's doublewide. It's neat, well-maintained, and securely locked. The rain hasn't yet washed away her garden. Doesn't look like anyone's looting, and let's hope it stays that way. Now we're heading to Mrs. Clayton's trailer, which is rundown and barely the size of a camper. Kevin's not going live from the park, but he's getting everything on video, when he's not wiping rain and debris off his lens.

Lizzie knocks on Mrs. Clayton's door. Silence. Whoever's inside may not have heard us over the wind. It's howling and whipping around tree limbs. Lizzie tries the handle. It turns, and she steps inside, then jumps back.

"She has a gun," Lizzie warns us.

I call in, "Mrs. Clayton. Your friend Mary Anne sent us to check on you. Are you all right?"

"Get the hell out of here!"

"Mrs. Clayton—"

"I will shoot."

***

LIZZIE

We don't know what to do. Then the wind decides for us. A towering pine tree crashes right on top of the trailer, flattening the back half.

Nick runs inside. A shot's fired. I scream. And then he staggers out, carrying a woman who has to be in her eighties, wearing a ragged nightie and hollering curses. I want to strangle her, but Mrs. Clayton is clearly crazy, or at least crazed. If Mr. Clayton isn't dead, he must've gotten the hell out of there long ago.

Kevin is capturing all of this, so he can't help. I join Nick, who thank goodness wasn't hit, trying to calm Mrs. Clayton, and get kicked in the shins. The woman's not wearing shoes, but her toes are like talons. That really hurt.

So here we are. Nick's not supposed to even be here, and he's the hero of the story. Mrs. Clayton is supposed to be a sad victim, and she's attacking us like a banshee. The pine tree missed our live truck by inches. And now, look at what's inside our truck.

As we're dragging Mrs. Clayton to safety, we see that Kevin left the door ajar, or more likely it blew open. And cowering on the driver's seat is a mutt. Drenched to the bone, shivering, panting, gazing at Nick with saucer eyes, even Mrs. Clayton's torrent of profanity doesn't budge this dog. Nick puts Mrs. Clayton in the passenger seat. The dog growls a little when Kevin tries lifting her off his seat, but she licks Nick as soon as he takes her in his arms.

We get back to the school and back on the air. Kevin feeds his video of the Clayton rescue—she's vowing to sue—and Bob broadcasts it raw and unedited, except for all the bleeps covering Mrs. Clayton's curses.

Hurricane Nyla does massive damage to South Florida. Especially, and so unfairly, to poor communities like Homestead, while Brickell Avenue lives to tremble another day. But miraculously, and it truly is a miracle, not a single life is lost.

As for the mutt… no chip, no tags. And no one comes forward to claim her even though our video is shown all over the world and endlessly shared on YouTube.

So for the first time in his life, Nick has a dog. And of course, we name her Nyla.

35

NICK

The hurricane raked South Florida for less than a day. The cleanup's taken three weeks so far, with no end in sight.

At Lizzie's insistence, I work with Karen on countless Help Center stories. We rarely do them as separate packages. WTAN and the other stations blew out network and syndicated programming during the first two weeks of the storm's aftermath. Local news still takes up most of the afternoon, and expands coverage each evening to cover the tens of thousands of people left homeless, including families like the ones we saw in Homestead, reduced to sleeping in their cars or trucks to protect what little they have left. Of the folks lucky enough to still have homes, one and a half million lost electricity. And most are still wringing out their waterlogged belongings.

Nyla destroyed thousands of businesses, including Bermuda Blues. Thankfully, Ardis has flood insurance. And speaking of that, the insurance companies sending reps to Homestead are heroic. They set up folding tables and chairs at makeshift tent cities, and cut checks to people who lost all their identification, simply taking their word that they had coverage so families can get money to live on. Leland Davis tells me, on camera, that a bunch of the smaller insurers are going to go bankrupt. They deserve recognition, and Bob Beardsley is making sure they get it.

Many other companies, though, are beneath contempt. Every day, the AG's office is exposing price gouging for water, generators, and other necessities. And we're now prosecuting.

As for builders, Lizzie is up on a roof right now.

***

LIZZIE

Suppose it's too late to mention that I'm afraid of heights as well as sharks. But Bob has me scampering on the few house roofs around Homestead that remain intact, to show how some builders saved money—pennies—by using fewer nails than required by code. Their negligence helped Nyla blow roofs to kingdom come. And without a roof, many of these homes blew apart.

"Who knew about this?" a furious Charlie Metz asks me.

He's a father of three, standing with his wife, Becky, and the kids next to a pile of timber that used to be their ranch house.

"I'm telling everyone watching." Charlie chokes back tears, pointing at Kevin's camera with a hammer. "You'd better climb up on a ladder and nail those shingles down yourself right now, before the next storm hits."

***

NICK

Help Center volunteers like Matthew and Alex, temporarily homeless themselves, are fielding calls from people who still have phone service. And then I go out, or general assignment reporters like Lizzie do, always armed with as many cases of water as we can fit in our vans. We're getting reinforcements—staff and supplies—from stations as far away as New York, Dallas, and Denver. Sometimes it's great to be part of a network.

***

LIZZIE

Yesterday morning, Kev and I showed how children are going back to class despite thirty-one schools needing to be totally rebuilt. The one we visited converted a cinderblock garage for the school's landscaping equipment, into four partitioned classrooms. The fourth- and fifth-graders there seemed a lot more attentive than I would've guessed. Maybe they've been scared into studiousness. But one of them, a boy who needed a clean pair of jeans and who knows what else, used a novel and sad excuse for not getting his homework done.

"We still don't have any lights, and Mom wouldn't let me use a candle because my sister almost burned the house down last night. Honest."

My mom offered to fly down to help fellow teachers, but none of the administrators I talked with are prepared to take her up on it. Instead, Mom and Dad and a lot of their neighbors are volunteering with a wonderful disaster relief organization in Cincinnati, gathering and packing up canned food, toiletries, clothing, you name it. Then other volunteers drive the stuff down here in trucks. So far, they've delivered more than twenty containers—370,000 pounds—of aid. These numbers, I know, are hard to digest. So try this one—two hundred. Right now, we're following trappers armed with nets and tranquilizer guns. They're rounding up two hundred residents who made a break from Monkey Jungle. Nick, your old friend the chimp may be coming for you.

"All of which is to say, between the gougers and the looters, and now, these other primates, it's a jungle out here. But good people are making a difference. Back to you, Karen and John."

<u>36</u>

LIZZIE

Finally, in time for Christmas, some normalcy is being restored. Including to my neck of the woods. After road crews cleared away all the toppled palm trees and brush that made it impossible even to approach our complex on Brickell Avenue, Meg, Ardis, and I discovered that—whew—our apartment suffered almost no damage. The girls stayed for a week with Harry's family. Jupiter was hardly hit at all. Daniela and her daughter escaped early and drove up to a hotel in Orlando. I was most worried about Mr. Falcone, but a kind member of his parish took in our old friend.

And now we're all back home. DeAndre even put up a Christmas tree in our lobby. It's pink metal, flocked with silver, and festooned with shiny green balls. Ah. We'll always have Miami.

I feel so much at home, that Nick and I invited Bob and Jan Beardsley over tonight to dinner. They accepted, and then Bob asked if he could bring a friend. This isn't like him. Bob is often mysterious, but he never lacks manners. So we know something must be up.

Hearing that I'm going to entertain for the first time since the storm, Nick's mom—whose mansion lost a bunch of roof tiles, and that's it, because it's built like a fortress—offered to send something over with Nick. Turns out to be a large tuna casserole.

"Mom made it herself. No help from Marianne. I'm supposed to tell you, in case anyone asks, that it has," being a nerd, Nick consults a card, "creamy avocado sauce, penne pasta, and red pepper. All you have to do is heat it up. And no thanks are needed. Mom asked you to think of it as potluck."

This is not potluck. It's charity, for me and our guests. And I'm grateful.

At seven on the dot, Tito announces the Beardsleys. Nick and I wait for them out in the hall. And guess who's the mystery plus-one?

Sheryl MacDonald.

I hug her for the first time and she hugs me back.

Sheryl says she followed our coverage, starting with Mrs. Clayton trying to kill us, and that it's been "courageous, compassionate, and I can't think of another compliment with a 'C'. Bravo, you."

I wouldn't normally quote a compliment, but coming from Sheryl MacDonald this means a lot.

Nick asks how she's doing. One thing I love about Nick is that he always steers conversations to another person. Sheryl tells us that she's working with a big Canadian broadcasting company that's starting a new cable channel.

"It's going to be called the Help Channel. And—"

Nick interrupts. "Sweetheart,is something burning?"

We all sniff, and then I'm about to call the fire department because something in my kitchen is getting incinerated. I run to find out what, open the oven, and there's the tuna casserole, looking like a zombie from one of my horror movies. The smoke sets off the alarm. I don't know how to turn it off! Bob slides open the door to the balcony. I want to toss the casserole off the balcony, but Nick stops me. Sheryl is choking. And finally Jan shuts off the broiler.

"Honey," Jan whispers, more compassionately than anything in my hurricane stories, "when you want to reheat something, better to use the oven than the broiler."

"I didn't know there was a difference." Oh, God, I'm back to blurting things out. While I'm at it, "Nick, don't tell your mother!"

He's doubled-over with laughter. I like him better stiff.

"Okay, here's what we'll do," my suddenly masterful boyfriend informs everyone. Did Ardis foresee this, too? "I'm going to order a couple pizzas. What do you like?"

Everyone tells him. I'm going to eat salad. They all try to make me feel better, which makes me feel worse. But at least the smoke is clearing, and I plead with DeAndre not to call the fire department or EMS.

Bob asks Sheryl to resume what she was saying about this new Help Channel. For a long, tall Texan, he has a terrible poker face.

Sheryl says, "I was able to show the executive producers several of your Help Center pieces, including the ones about the weaselly dance instructor and the poor family getting ripped off by the grocery store. They'd already seen your first night of hurricane coverage. Everyone has. How is that old lady, by the way?"

"She's still suing us for saving her life," Bob says.

We all laugh, except Nick, who really could've been killed.

"So here's the offer," Sheryl says.

At the word *offer,* Nick and I sit bolt upright in surprise.

"How would you two like to star in your own network show called *The HelpMates*?"

Silence. We're stunned. I look at Nick. He looks at me. We both stare at Sheryl.

And then I look at Bob Beardsley. "You're behind this, of course. Won't you get in trouble if Nick and I up and leave WTAN?"

"Nope," Bob says. "Because there's something you don't know, that I didn't want anyone to know until we got past the worst of this hurricane. The day before it hit, the day Steve Rosser came down here and started throwing his weight around, and well, you know everything he did. The day Rosser came down, I handed in my resignation. And he was happy to accept it. Then all hell broke loose and all of us had to pitch in. For the station and the community. This community has been good to all of us, even if the network hasn't always been. Anyway, I'm not behind this Help Channel. I'm not going to be part of anything. I'm sixty-eight years old and my bride and I are going home to Waco."

Jan takes his hand.

"But," and this is turning out to be quite a speech from Bob Beardsley, "when Sheryl told me what she was up to, and asked for a little advice, I reminded her that she has two future stars right here in Miami. And she said—"

"Don't I know it," Sheryl finishes.

"Her exact words," Bob says.

"By the way," Sheryl adds, "*HelpMates* doesn't necessarily mean you're married. Just that you're—"

"Matey," Jan says.

And we all laugh.

The pizza arrives. I have three slices of pepperoni and no salad. Then we take a stroll under the stars, by the bay, Bob and Jan holding hands, Sheryl MacDonald with her arms around Nick and me.

<u>37</u>

LIZZIE

Nick gave notice to Leland Davis. The attorney general said all the right things, and according to Nick, even seemed to mean some of them. Another assistant AG will be assigned to WTAN and they won't miss a beat.

Since Bob remains in charge of our newsroom for now, I gave formal notice to him. My contract has a non-compete clause, but that only keeps me from working for other stations in Miami and Fort Lauderdale. The clause includes an *out* for networks, including cable. Bob assures me there won't be a problem. There's no shortage of people who will be as grateful as I was—and as grateful as I remain to Bob and Sheryl—for having the chance to work for this fine station in this great market.

Now there's only one thing left to do. We have to tell Karen. Both of us.

It's not like we haven't talked. In fact, Karen's become a whole new person since the hurricane. Besides anchoring every evening, seven nights a week, my sister's thrown herself into covering all kinds stories in the field. My favorite, because it included Harry Mattis, followed a battery of Marines storming Miami Gardens and making like the guys at Iwo Jima raising the flag, except this time they were rebuilding the demolished home of a retired gunnery sergeant. Karen used photos and film clips to show how the now eighty-year-old Sergeant Major James Powell earned the Medal of Honor in Vietnam, scaling a concrete wall during an enemy barrage to move wounded troops to safety. But there was nothing solemn about Kary's report. Sergeant Powell, Harry, and all the heroes were funny as hell, whacking their thumbs with hammers while showing the Powell great-grandkids how real men do carpentry. Then seven-year-old Taneisha Powell pulled a toy hammer out of her tool belt and showed how it's really done. Karen did all her stories without a producer and made friends everywhere she went.

With one exception. Steve Rosser.

Here's what I pieced together from Karen, Bob Beardsley, and Sheryl MacDonald. As soon as Sheryl was fired, Rosser made his move. He'd been friends for years with Sheryl's replacement, Fred Arhaus, and Rosser convinced him that, rather than firing Karen, it would be better for the network to rehabilitate her at one of Rosser's O and O's.

It's too mustache-twirling to suggest that Steve Rosser had lusted after Kary ever since she joined the network, but it's true. And that isn't surprising. Look how Nick was drooling. All right, I promised him not to bring that up again. Anyway, Rosser and Arhaus approached Kary, and she agreed moving to Miami would be best.

At first, she resisted taking over the Help Center, but Rosser assured my sister that I'd be thrilled to do weekend morning anchoring. All Rosser knew about Kary and Nick was that they'd been college classmates. Had he known how intimate they were, Rosser never would have pushed the Help Center idea. Need proof? How's this. When Rosser moved Kary into a room at the InterContinental Hotel until she found a permanent place to live, he took the adjoining room, separated only by a door that didn't have to remain locked. Rosser knew that Kary had broken up with Kwami Thomas. He was hoping her door would be open.

But Rosser didn't know Karen Lomax. My sister had fended off a handsy news director in Houston, and an even more aggressive field producer in Iraq—one reason she insisted on working with Lisa Nape instead of another male producer. I don't know how blatant Steve Rosser was. Kary didn't want to talk about it. But she threatened to sue if Rosser didn't move out of that hotel and communicate with her only through Bob Beardsley.

Karen regrets not filing that lawsuit, especially when she learned that Rosser next moved in on Ileana Bonilla, the reporter whose mother was ill over Thanksgiving. Ileana is now weighing her options.

Kary, understandably, is still at the InterContinental, in a luxury suite on the club level. Where are you going to move a month after

Hurricane Nyla? She could make a fortune subletting a corner of her hotel room to a family of five.

It's now 10 a.m., three days after Sheryl MacDonald came to my place for dinner and made her offer, which I still can't believe. Nick and I each resigned yesterday. Otherwise, we haven't spoken with anyone about this, not even our parents. Not even Meg or Harry. Certainly not Ardis, who would charter one of those planes that fly over Miami Beach with banners. Bless her.

"Want to go down for breakfast?" my sister asks. "Or I can order something up here."

We decline. Kary's in a great mood. Her work has been first-rate and our ratings are sky-high. I haven't seen her this happy in years, even when she was snagging scoops like that exclusive with Duchess Meghan.

"This was such a good idea, Liz." She plops down on a sectional sofa that's actually a lot like mine, except it's white.

Despite having maid service, Kary's managed to make this place messy.

"We're all running around so much," she says. "I feel like I saw you more in New York, on the Sunday Skyping. And, oh, I'm supposed to tell you, Mom and Dad say you look fabulous. That sounds bad. Like you're on *ET*. You're out there helping so many people—"

"We all are," I say. "It's what we get to do."

"Yes. And you know…" Karen looks down for a moment. "It's terrible to say, because so many people are still suffering, and it sounds like Journalism one-O-one, but this is why I got into the business. Why you did, too, Liz. And Nick, you're a big part of this as well. What everyone's been doing, the volunteers, the photographers, all of us. It means more to me than what I did at *Backstory*. What I got credit for at *Backstory*."

"And blame," I remind her. "Unfairly."

"It wasn't unfair. Karen says. "I didn't want to admit it, but my name was on that story. I should've been more involved. Lisa Nape and I talked last week for the first time since she got fired. She's now an executive producer in Minneapolis. That's where she's from, so they know her. She said the technical expert was absolutely sure the fuel tanks in those trucks were dangerous. But they couldn't make them explode in a crash test, even after three tries. And Lisa assured *Backstory* that we'd have the story for the start of sweeps. So..."

We say nothing, which I hope doesn't seem like criticism, because I understand. You can't condone it, but I understand.

"Anyway." Karen laughs. "As usual, I'm monopolizing the conversation. How are you doing?"

I realize that Karen seems to take it for granted that *you* means Nick and me, together, even though we're no longer working together. And Karen seems happy about that, too. That we're together.

But is she? And why the hell should it matter? I know Nick Harris loves me. The guy risked his life in a hurricane and looked down the barrel of a gun to be with me when he was supposed to be taking my sister to a ball. What my sister had planned for them, I don't want to think about. It shouldn't matter. But a lifetime of feeling I could never measure up to my sister keeps me wondering if he's still dazzled by her. So I can't help asking.

"How are we doing, Nick? I'd like you to tell me, here in front of my sister."

"Sweetheart, I'm happy to tell your sister. And your parents, as I've already told my family. I love you. You are the love of my life. Anything that happened before—"

"So long ago," Karen adds.

"When Karen and I dated for two months—"

"I don't know if it was even that long," Karen says.

"... back in college," Nick never takes his eyes off me, "seven years before I first saw you on TV and developed the same crush half the guys in this city have—"

"It would be all the guys," Karen says, "but half of them are gay."

"... and eight years before I finally got to meet you—"

"As you were staring at my sister on TV," I remind him. The hell with that promise.

"... and I took you to lunch—"

"At the Biltmore," Karen reminds me.

"... and watched you rough up con-artists and crooks," Nick smiles, "and took you dancing, and took you to my mother's house, and took you—"

"All right," I say. "We don't have to get into that."

"And I realized," Nick embraces me, "we may be hungry for the rest of our lives because you can't cook, and I can't either, but that I'd rather be hungry with you—"

"Than be full eating with your mother," I finish for him. "That doesn't sound as romantic as I hoped."

"Lizzie," Karen says, seriously. "This is your insecurity talking. Which I have *never* understood. Did Nick and I once have feelings? Sometimes one weekend with a guy in college can make you feel you've met the love of your life. But honestly—"

"Please don't be brutally honest." Nick laughs.

"It was a crush," Karen says. "Can you blame anyone for crushing on Nick?"

He blushes. I've never seen him blush before. Hardly anyone blushes in Miami because they're so tan. And based on the Help Center complaints, so shameless.

Karen asks, "Didn't you have any crushes like that, Lizzie?"

It's sad that my own sister doesn't know. So I remind her.

"Sure. Rob Pattinson, in *Twilight*. But that's different. He really is coming back for me, and being a vampire, unlike Nicholas, Rob will always look the same."

"Well," Nick says, "Karen will be relieved to know that I'm not coming back for her. Because, Elizabeth Katherine Lomax, I love you with all my heart. And I always will."

We kiss. It's even better than the ones in the darkened studio.

Then Nick says, "Do you want me to tell your sister?"

"What?" Karen asks.

I announce, "We're leaving. The station."

"For where?"

"You can't tell anyone yet, Kary, but we've been offered, together, the chance to do a show. On a new cable channel. And… that's it. We're going to do it."

Karen has her hands over her mouth. I don't know what's going to come out. When it comes to career and ambition, I've learned that my sister is not the person I want to be.

But thankfully, she shouts, "That's wonderful. I'm so happy for you. Have you told Mom?"

"Not yet. She'll go viral, single-handedly, and we're not supposed to say anything yet."

"And when are you two getting married?"

Both our mouths hang open.

"Oh, come on," Karen says. "Even John McIntyre knows you're getting married, and he didn't know that Prince Harry married Meghan."

"You'll be the first to know," I say.

"Okay," Kary says to Nick, "if you want my father never to speak to you again. Dad's the family romantic. Tell him and our mom first. Tell me second."

And my big sister kisses us both.

EPILOGUE

LIZZIE and **NICK**

We're back at the Biltmore for our wedding day, not coincidentally one year to the day after Nick first took me here for lunch.

Unlike that day last year, Lizzie and I have a lot more people than Bernard the waiter to talk with.

Although, for old times' sake, Bernard will be serving us at the bride and groom's table. We can't name everyone who's coming, but where to start?

Well, how about your girlfriends? Harry's bringing Ardis.

And Harry is going to sing one of Nick's songs. A new one written for me. It's called "Help Me Share the Love." Help. Get it? They haven't let me hear it yet, but Ardis says it's beautiful, and she's a tough audience.

Speaking of Ardis, Bermuda Blues has really taken off after the insurance money let Ardis and Kim fix it up even nicer than before.

And Ardis, of course, found me my wedding gown.

A mermaid gown. It's magical. They'll be sitting with Meg and... who is she bringing?

A guy named Reggie. He plays sax on some of her cruises. We're taking a four-night cruise with Meghan tomorrow.

But our longer honeymoon's going to be in the spring.

In Paris. I finally get to see Paris.

My cousin Howie is also at that table. With a date, so Aunt Sue won't spend the reception hunting for a future daughter-in-law.

Hope Uncle Marty doesn't lecture the girl about how everyone's now waiting 'til they're on Medicare to start a family.

Are we going to wait that long?

Let's see how the wedding goes. And the honeymoon.

Kevin is sitting at that table, too. He's by himself, maybe hoping to meet someone.

Your cousin Sandi is cute. Then there's a Help Center table with Daniela and her daughter, Paola. And Lucy, Matthew, Alex, Lenny, Joel, and Shirley, and... Ivy Lewis and her son Lamar. I love that they're coming. But no, not Aunt Alicia. She's never forgiven me.

There was nothing to forgive. Alicia, the anchor Alicia, is coming. In case you don't know, she's was scooped up right away by the guys at WTAN's biggest competitor.

And Alicia's giving Karen a run for her money.

Bob Beardsley and Jan came back from Texas.

Just for the wedding.

And Lizzie and I have a standing invitation to visit them in Waco.

We're going to take them up on that. Nicholas and I are still based here in Miami, but HelpMates *does stories all over the country.*

And outside the country. Hope you catch our investigation of a Russian adoption ring.

Someone who won't be attending our wedding—who's going nowhere—is Steve Rosser.

A national exposé proved that Rosser pressured female reporters from LA to New York to have sex.

One of those reporters was Ileana Bonilla. She's now suing, and Kary says she'll testify. But UBN isn't waiting for the courts. Both Rosser and his henchman, Harry Lutz, are out on their asses, and the network will settle. Big time. After all the coverage, I don't think either of those reptiles will ever work in the business again. So let's be grateful other women are now protected.

At least from them.

And let's think about something more fun. The local paper did a Sunday magazine cover story about us last week.

Lizzie looked almost as beautiful as she looks today.

It's about time for you to stop looking so I can squeeze into that dress. The point is, we're blessed. My parents are well. Dad discovered that your mom likes Hallmark movies, too. And you have to see them discussing their favorites.

Including their favorite weddings. Don't the couples in those movies always get married at the end?

They'd better. Your grandma also seems to enjoy them. Now Kary and I need to persuade Mom and Dad to retire and move down here. Karen's happier at WTAN than she's ever been. And she's back with Kwami.

Hope he makes it to the ceremony. The whole staff wants his autograph. Harry Mattis and I are starting a campaign to get Kwami traded to the Heat.

And then if all that happens, you know what, sweetheart? Everyone we love, including our ring bearer—

Nyla, our dog—

... will be here with us, in Miami.

ABOUT THE AUTHOR

After graduating from Yale and Columbia, Jack Atherton practiced law in Manhattan for seven years before becoming a TV anchor and reporter. He and his wife, Aymsley, and their two daughters, spent five years in Miami, which they love.

CONNECT WITH JACK:

website: RealJackAtherton.com
facebook: facebook.com/jack.atherton.9480
twitter: @jackatherton111
instagram: @Anchormanjack

www.BOROUGHSPUBLISHINGGROUP.com

If you enjoyed this book, please write a review. Our authors appreciate the feedback, and it helps future readers find books they love. We welcome your comments and invite you to send them to info@boroughspublishinggroup.com. Follow us on Facebook, Twitter and Instagram, and be sure to sign up for our newsletter for surprises and new releases from your favorite authors.

Are you an aspiring writer? Check out www.boroughspublishinggroup.com/submit and see if we can help you make your dreams come true.

Made in the USA
Monee, IL
29 June 2020